A Very Dominant Woman

Lady Alexa

This novel is a work of fiction. Names, characters, businesses, places, events and incidents are either the products of the author's imagination or used in a fictitious manner. Any resemblance to actual persons, living or dead, or actual events is purely coincidental.

This erotic novel contains scenes of a sexual nature including male to female gender transformation, sexual acts, forced feminisation, CFNM, humiliation and female domination.

Strictly for adult readers aged 18+ only.

Read more Forced Feminisation, FLR and Femdom.

Subscribe to my real-life forced feminisation and FLR blog and Newsletter at:

ladyalexauk.com

Part 1

A Dominant Lady's Story

Chapter 1

The natural order

It’s a woman’s role to feminise and humiliate men. This was the rule according to Aretta Ademola.

A man entering Aretta's world had to live with her philosophy of female superiority. Aretta never failed in her objective to subjugate a man once she identified her target. Men were better as submissive girls in her eyes.

That day, Aretta was relaxing in her home. She gazed out from a black leather armchair that seemed to surround her like a womb. Her vast contemporary penthouse apartment was in the

Barrio de Salamanca, the smartest district in Madrid Spain.

The room was a large area of tiled floor and sparse glossy furniture in brilliant white. It was pristine and ordered as Aretta expected it to be. The sound violins swept through the room like a swirling classical roller-coaster from discretely hidden speakers.

Her black laptop lay open on the dining room table. The light from its logo cast a dull glow on the table's top. She had finished working through the document that lay open on the screen. The furniture was top of the range. She had earned the right to have the best, she was the best in her field. Aretta had a steely determination to succeed in everything. Including the domination of men.

"Does Mistress Ademola need anything?" Her housemaid's voice fought against the volume of the violins filling each corner of the room.

Aretta looked up from her smartphone. She had been reading an email. The phone's screen lit up her square ebony face. She shook her head from side to side, her thick red lips pursed. Long wavy black hair flicked across the ops of her bare muscular shoulders. There was no smile with the negative response.

Her stony face hid the satisfaction at her maid using her surname with her title: Mistress. Respect, that's what she demanded from her maids, it wasn't much to ask for. Their total obedience.

She peered at her maid imperiously. The maid's blond hair was too light to be its natural colour. It was full-bodied and rested on wide shoulders. Despite this, the maid had a long thin slender body. Silver drop earrings caught the light through the maid's hair.

Aretta's eyes glared like searchlights as her maid's eyes lowered to the floor. The maid knew not to seek direct eye contact with the Mistress. Aretta's mouth twitched into the beginnings of a smile of satisfaction. She loved to see her housemaids dressed in tight black satin dresses. Their smooth hairless light-skinned arms and bodies looked out of place with their oversized breasts.

There was a frill on each side of the shoulder of the dress. A brilliant white pinafore hung around the maid's waist. The dress flared out from the maid's waist. It was so short, it barely covered the pink frilled knickers beneath it.

The dress did not cover the frilly stocking tops. An area of bare chalky-white flesh was on show between the panties and the stocking tops. Smooth pale skin was broken by silky black suspender belt straps. A white starchy petticoat showed below the hem of the little dress, it rustled every time the maid moved.

Aretta’s eyes fell down the maid’s body towards the long exposed legs in patterned black stockings. White flesh peeked through the open diagonal shapes on the stockings. The maid’s black leather shoes had high heels. The thin stiletto heels gave an undeserved elegance to the maid's slender legs.

The maid hadn’t always been willowy, it had taken Aretta’s strict training programme to make it so.

The maid waited to be dismissed, eyes swivelling one way and the other and showing discomfort. The maid had worn this dress style ever since starting to work for Aretta over eighteen months ago. It was not negotiable. The maid could do nothing but endure the humiliation because the consequences of not doing so were worse.

Aretta waved the maid away with disdain. She returned to her work on her smartphone.

Relief passed across the maid's face. After a deep curtsey, there was a drop of the head with eyes fixed on the floor. Aretta did not acknowledge the submissive gesture but she saw it from the edge of her vision. She was satisfied. Aretta missed nothing.

"Wait," ordered Aretta. She stood, a hand on the remote control winding the music volume down low. She put her face two inches from her housemaid's face. Aretta smelled the harsh cheap perfume over the top of her own expensive brand.

The large pores on the housemaid's face were not fully hidden by a layer of light foundation. The maid blinked smoky dark-grey eyelids and long false eyelashes.

Aretta put a finger to her maid's face and ran it along a strong jawline. "I can feel stubble, Polly." Aretta's face darkened. "How many times do I have to tell you I want your face smooth. You are a girl and girl's have a smooth face."

Aretta never raised her voice, her assured authoritative manner made that unnecessary.

She stared with disgust at the maid. He lowered his head and screwed his eyes.

The maid cringed, his eyes fixed on an imaginary spot on the wall waiting for the inevitable punishment. He didn't know how to respond, he had been sure he had shaved smoothly. He had used a five-blade wet razor razor in the morning and again in the afternoon. He must have missed a bit; careless. Mistress Aretta missed nothing.

"I cannot trust you, girl. This means electrolysis. I will have your facial hair removed permanently. Polly, you are a useless sissy." Her tone dripped with anger and menace. "Anyway, electrolysis is better for the best in the long run." Aretta sighed loudly at the inconvenience of having to arrange this.

“I'm sorry, Mistress, I thought.”

She cut him off with a long elegant hand against his lips, leaving his protestation hanging in the air.

“I have no wish to listen to your snivelling excuses, sissy.” She slapped him around his face, a loud spank echoed in the room. He put a hand to his reddened cheek, his eyes wide with anguish. His long pink nails pressed against an inflamed cheek.

“Stand in the corner, stupid, with your panties around your ankles. Then place your hands on your head.” Aretta flicked her fingers together twice to snap him into action.

Polly bent down and pulled his panties to his ankles. He waddled to the corner with tiny steps, his chastity cage and bare loose balls swung as he walked. A grin swept over Aretta's face at the sight of his desperation to follow her orders. She loved seeing his difficulty in walking in stiletto heels and ankles bound by panties.

"Candy," Aretta called out. A second maid tottered from the kitchen area dressed identically to Polly and with the same hairstyle.

He curtsied, asking how he could serve.

"Get me the large wooden spoon," said Aretta.

He curtsied but his eyes showed apprehension as they swept across to see his colleague Polly in the corner. He disappeared back into the kitchen. Polly was standing, looking worried. He faced a corner of the apartment, his frilly pink panties hung around his ankles, his knees touched.

The short dress exposed the bottom of the cheeks of a taut naked bottom. A luminous pink rubber flange showed against his cheeks. A butt plug. The plug was five inches long but she would soon be switching it for one of six inches. Aretta insisted her sissies were plugged.

Candy returned from the kitchen with a twelve-inch long wooden spoon. He glanced at Polly again before handing the spoon to his mistress. Aretta grabbed the spoon, her blue eyes sparkled with restrained anger.

Aretta strode to Polly with the spoon held high. “Bend.”

He turned to one side and bent over.

She crashed the spoon down on his bottom cheeks with a whack. Polly jumped with the impact. It left a spoon-shaped red welt on his bottom cheek. She followed up nine further times, each time Polly's body jerked with the stinging pain.

Once finished, she pulled him up by his hair. She spun him around to face her. They were eye to eye. She lifted the front of his dress with her dark slender hand exposing the pink plastic chastity cage. A small golden padlock glinted.

Aretta lifted his caged penis to expose his hairless balls. She brought the wooden spoon down on them with a loud slap. He stifled a scream and tears came into his eyes. Mascara ran down the cheeks of his face in thin lines.

"Turn back into the corner and stay there until I tell you to leave," she said. She breathed out hard with impatience. She mumbled to herself about having to be forever managing and controlling her girls. "What do you have to say to me, sissy?"

"Thank you for your punishment, Mistress. I deserved it." His head was bowed, panties crumpled around his slim ankles.

Aretta went to a black leather sofa and sat-. Her leather trouser outfit matched the sofa. She picked up her phone again. The sharp white light reflected off her deep blue eyes, the eyes that ensnared everyone. She looked at the time on the phone screen. It was after 9 pm, time for dinner.

She got up and walked to the dining area. She sat at a long smoked-glass table with x-shaped wooden legs. Outside, the lights from the city's buildings twinkled through the floor-to-ceiling picture window.

She clicked her fingers. "Candy, bring me

my dinner and a glass of wine. I will have the Château de Beaune, 2012." She glared at him. "And make sure it is at exactly 16 degrees C."

A voice came from the kitchen among the clanging noises. "Yes, Mistress Ademola, right away."

"Males are such bores when allowed to think or have opinions," she said out loud. "A feminised sissy man is the only way they understand. I am right am I not, Polly?"

Polly shook in the corner. "Yes, Mistress Ademola."

The swish of Candy's petticoat told Aretta her dinner was arriving. He served her a salad dish and a plate of mixed seafood. He set down a wine glass and poured the red wine halfway up as she liked it.

He stood back and curtsied. “Enjoy your meal, Mistress Ademola.”

She grunted. All men were weak, without exception. She held many women in contempt too. Not for their weaknesses like men because women were strong. No, she believed many women never understood or used their genetic superiority and never used it.

Aretta ruffled feathers but it was accepted by those around her due to her success. She had few friends but many admirers.

Heads turned everywhere Aretta went. Not only for her regal beauty, but her regal demeanour. She looked like a queen and she acted like one. She was the queen ruling in the court of feeble males.

Chapter 2

Becoming a dominant woman

Aretta Ademola was one of the most successful women in Spain. At just 32, she was Vice-President of Marketing for Spain's most successful range of cosmetics brands. It had not always been that way.

As a six-year-old child, she arrived in Spain from Nigeria with her single mother. They'd escaped from a bad father and terrible husband. They settled in a poor district in a backward province of Spain. It was all they could afford. The locals had never seen anyone like Aretta before. Tall with deep brown ski, her steel-blue eyes shone with defiance and a profound and calculating intelligence.

Her mother made the same mistakes as she had back in Africa, spurred on by desperation. She had a series of abusive, alcoholic and drug-addled boyfriends. It was not without reason Aretta developed a deep mistrust of men.

She learned from a young age about males. She watched, took everything in and stored it away. Aretta survived and thrived through a prodigious intellect and single-minded drive to succeed. And succeed she did, on her own terms. She needed no one. It was the only way for her.

Her school years were tough, to begin with. She was poorly dressed skinny unsmiling Aretta. And she was taller than the boys and didn't look anything like the other children. Initially, she couldn't speak Spanish. She became fluent inside four weeks.

Her name is synonymous with female success and achievement but when she was a child, the name Aretta Ademola seemed odd to the children of the district.

She was threw herself into her studies, her deep sparkling inquisitive intellect took her to the top of every class in every subject. On the sports field, she excelled; her once skinny body soon filled out into a muscular athletic build. Nothing was too difficult for Aretta even when dressed in old hand-me-down clothing.

The children were cruel, especially the boys. Some girls tried to befriend her, valuing her academic skills, but the cool girls ignored her to start with. Study wasn't cool, was it? They soon changed their minds. Aretta resolved that she would be the cool one but not a stupid uneducated cool one like these fools. She would be cool *and* well-educated. That was cool.

She was fourteen the day the boys changed their attitude towards her. Her body had spurted up and her muscles had grown through sports activities. Her voluminous breasts had begun to grow impressive.

One day, three boys ambushed her outside school. They pushed her too far, teasing her with racial and sexual taunts. They were cowards. She took on all three that day, leaving each of them lying on the floor, bloody and beaten.

Both sides learned a lesson. The boys never again taunted her and started to treat her with awe and respect. And she became aware of the physical power that went with her stunning intellect.

A butterfly had emerged from the gawky chrysalis of childhood. She now had the beauty, the brains and the power.

Instead of taunting her, the boys tried to impress her. She attracted them like bees around their queen. She never dated one single boy at the school. They were below her. She treated them with undisguised contempt. She noticed how this increased their ardour.

She observed and enjoyed the awakening of her power over feeble pathetic males. She hated their faked aggression and competition. The boys' belligerence and confidence fell away into docility and submission with her. This was fascinating to her. She loved this feeling and wanted more. It fed her newfound feeling: superiority. Not everyone had learned this yet.

As she approached fifteen, she decided it was time to test her power against one of her former tormentors: the school football captain, Sergio. He still retained a sense of his own superiority. The boys and girls all admired him in the school. The girls surrounded him and the boys followed him as their leader. Sergio was her rival.

He showed interest in her but he was too arrogant to chase her like the others. She bided her time until it was on her terms. One day, she spotted him practising football on his own at lunchtime on the sports field. She sauntered up to him. He stopped and looked at her without comment.

"Would you like a blow job, Sergio?"

"Yeah, sure, why not," he smirked back. His

confidence was complete. He was comfortable, he was the winner and her question confirmed it for him. She would kneel before him and give him pleasure. It was his destiny, he thought. He hadn't listened to her question properly.

Aretta led him to the edge of the playing field, her school bag over her shoulder. She was a head taller than Sergio. She led him behind the old thick gnarled trunk of an orange tree and told him to strip. A thin file of ants was stripping the remains of the fruit from this once mighty tree as she spoke.

He hesitated. "Why should I strip? You can suck my cock poking out through my flies."

"That is no fun," she said. "It would be better if you are naked."

He still hadn't listened properly to what she

was saying. She knew his arrogance would override his common-sense.

Sergio stripped, his concern about stripping naked was over-ridden by the promise of a blow job from the hottest girl in school. And his arrogance at his strong body. He stripped naked and place his clothes beside him. His erection was strong.

"Pass me your clothes," she said.

He hesitated again, his eyes said he knew something wasn't right. His hard desperate erection made the decision for him. He handed her his clothes. She placed them behind her.

Suddenly naked and defenceless, he urged her to get on with it and suck him off.

"Close your eyes, Sergio," she said.

He waited a short moment then screwed his

eyes closed.

Aretta picked up his clothes and walked away with them under her arm. He heard her footsteps crunch on the ground and opened his eyes horrified. His threw his hands down to cover his erection. He hid behind the old tree trunk.

"Come back." He shouting out at her from behind the cover of the tree. He cursed her.

She stopped and spun around, fifteen feet from the tree. His cries were attracting attention from those in the playground at the edge of the field.

"I asked if you wanted a blow job, Sergio. I never said I was going to give you one." She never smiled.

He pleaded again for his clothes.

"I cannot give you your clothes, Sergio."

"Why, why not?" His pleas were desperate.

She rested on one leg. "Say please and I will consider letting you put something on to return to the school buildings."

She had him defenceless. "Please, Aretta. Please, please," he said.

Aretta put his clothes down on the grass beside her and slipped the school bag off her shoulder. His head poked around the old tree trunk, watching. He kept his body hidden.

She removed a white girl's school blouse and a short blue-pleated gym skirt from the bag. Sergio's eyes widened in horror. He may not be bright, she thought, but even he could now see her plan. She laid out the skirt and the blouse on the grass beside her.

“You may put these on, Sergio.” She turned, picked up his male clothes and stuffed them in her bag. She strolled back to the end of the playing field by the school buildings.

She turned and watched the naked Sergio scamper from the tree with a hand over his penis. He ran to the little skirt and white blouse. He slipped them on and ran to the edge of the field, trying to use the bushes as cover.

Aretta called to the youngsters around her and pointed to Sergio. He ran hunched over, dressed in the short pleated skirt and blouse. The children laughed and pointed at him. Not Aretta. She remained calm as she felt her body growing with the power this humiliation gave her.

She held her head upright, her shoulders back. This was the first time she had feminised a male. It was exhilarating and liberating. She knew this would not be the last time.

She passed her school bag to a boy standing beside her. "Carry this, boy. Follow me."

He took it and scampered behind her. She no longer needed to carry anything herself. She had others to do that now.

Aretta matured into womanhood. She enjoyed selecting the occasional sexual partner or suffering a boyfriend when time permitted. The lessons she had learned from childhood and the suffering of her mother at the hands of men meant all relationships had to be on her terms. She was superior to these men. She knew that.

Her terms were simple: she was in charge of every decision, every element of any relationship, whether it was one night or longer. She enjoyed the conflict with some of the males who considered themselves alpha. She loved the tussle she always won. Her intensity and assertiveness ensured this happened every time.

Aretta had a gift. The tall skinny, strange looking immigrant girl from the backwaters had morphed into a woman every man desired. Her looks turned heads in the street from even the most stubborn men. They all acquiesced to her control and desires. Her thin lanky frame had transformed into a six-foot majestic lithe physique. Her skin was like smooth dark chocolate dark and her eyes were blue penetrating orbs of ice-cold steel.

She used forced feminisation and humiliation as her control mechanism. It gave her an intense sexual excitement. Sometimes, men were reluctant to be feminised to begin with, sometimes not. Every one of them succumbed.

Even the most outward alpha-macho types succumbed to her in the end. They all became submissive malleable sissy girls and housemaids under her control. Control and power fed her.

She knew men were predicable and their arrogance was a façade. Beneath their façade, they craved female dominance. Her female dominance. She had the power to make any man into a girlie or a sissy, a maid or a secretary, a slave or a plaything.

This is what life was about for Aretta Ademola. And she lived this life to the full.

Chapter 3

More power

Aretta waited by the white solid front door inside her apartment. It was a little after 7.30 in the morning. She was almost ready to leave for her working day at her company headquarters.

Polly stood at her side. He wore a white suit. The jacket was short and came in neatly at the waist. It had wide lapels. It was done up with two large white buttons. Polly squirmed in a figure-hugging mini pencil skirt. The bottom of his panties peeked out from below the hem. He tugged at it but there was no more length to find.

Aretta insisted her feminised male employees wear the tiniest skirts and dresses. She delighted in watching them squirm in discomfort, exposure and humiliation. It kept them vulnerable but looked damn good too.

Polly's black sheer stockings had a perfect straight dark line down the back. His black shoes had a small heel. This was better for driving; he was also her driver.

Polly's long flowing blond hair was pulled into a tight ponytail and tied with a pink ribbon in an oversized bow. His ears glistened with long diamanté earrings which jangled and glittered as he moved.

Polly removed Aretta's business jacket from the stand and held it out for her to put on. Aretta half smiled as she held her arms out backwards waiting for Polly to slip it over her arms. She never tired of seeing her submissives serving her. She shrugged it ober her slim muscular shoulders and her black business dress.

Polly bent to retrieve Aretta's handbag from a small hall table. Aretta watched his figure-hugging skirt ride up high to expose the bottom half of his bare bottom. The thin string of his g-string panties lay across the centre of a pink butt plug. She grinned to see his smooth balls separated by the g-string into separate sacks.

Polly looked up to see Aretta's smirk linger. He lowered his eyes instantly and stood, tugging his skirt down again. The shape of his cock cage was evident at the front.

Aretta's black dress went to just above her knees. Her long legs were bare and she wore black high-heeled shoes. She took great pride in her appearance and physique, a pride that was justified. Appearance was an important element of her ability to dominate people and situations. She was vain but didn't care, she had good reason to be vain.

Aretta Ademola – from gawky child to the sharpest sexiest executive in Europe.

Polly opened the front door and stepped back to allow Aretta to leave first. She stepped out with regal strides into the corridor. He followed and closed the door. A hoover started up from the apartment. Candy had begun his cleaning duties. Aretta insisted all cleaning be performed when she was out.

They made their way towards the lift entrance at the end of the corridor. The lift went to the underground car park. Polly carried his mistress's bag. Aretta didn't carry things.

They walked toeiwards the lift, Aretta leading.

They passed an elderly female resident, her hair was unnaturally black, her make-up heavy. She muttered *buenos dias* at them. Her mouth dropped open at seeing Polly and a dawning realisation fell over her; Polly was not what *she* seemed at first glance. Polly looked down and a red flush appeared on his neck. Aretta nodded a curt polite reply.

They got in the waiting lift and descended to the basement. Aretta strode first from the lift to her long sleek black Mercedes. The faint odour of oil permeated the car park area. Aretta waited by the car. Black. It was her favourite colour.

Polly opened the rear door, lowered his head and curtsied. He placed a leg forward and a leg extended behind him. His skirt rose again to expose the chastity cage shaped bulge as his g-string panties. Aretta ducked into the car. She glanced around the interior, the smell of new leather filled her nostrils. She permitted herself a smile once again at her success. He never took it for granted.

She watched with self-satisfied pride as Polly slid into the driver's seat. His blond ponytail with a pink-bowed ribbon bobbed as he settled. He started the car and pulled out of the car park and up and into the snarled streets of Madrid's rush-hour traffic. Aretta was already working on emails on her smartphone.

Within thirty minutes, they had arrived at the shimmering towers of Madrid's business district. Polly slowed the car and indicated a left turn by a ten-story white-stoned building. It had been built in a facsimile of traditional Spanish style but completed only eighteen months ago.

Polly drove the large saloon into an access road by the side of the building. He turned onto a steep concrete ramp which took them into an underground car park beneath the office block. He parked in the bay labelled:

Reservado

La Señora Ademola, Vice Presidente.'

Once parked, Polly jumped out and tugged his tiny tight skirt down to cover his panties as best he could. He went round to Aretta's door. He pulled down the hem of his short pencil skirt again as he walked. Just walking made the skirt rise, exposing his skimpy pink panties.

He yearned for a longer skirt but knew the

answer. He opened Aretta's door with a small curtsey. He held the hem of his skirt this time to avoid it rising too far. His long black false eyelashes fluttered as he swept a furtive glance around the ill-lit underground space.

Aretta was pleased his hair had grown long rather than when he first had to wear a wig. She preferred her maids to have their own feminine hairstyle. Wigs were never ideal as they allowed the male to revert to a male look.

She never tired of seeing her success and power to feminise and humiliate men. She smirked as she watched Polly's discomfort. His eyes dart around the basement car park hoping there was no one around. Aretta felt a tingle in her stomach and dampness forming in her panties at her power to make this happen.

Her power stimulated her. Polly was a pathetic creature with a small penis she kept permanently caged. Sometimes she allowed him and his sissy friend, Candy, to milk each other. That was amusing, especially as she made them drink each other's after. Wonderful, she thought.

As Aretta stepped out of the car, Polly maintained his lowered curtsy position until she was clear. She studied his face and stroked his jawline. He had a smooth face today.

"Good girl," she whispered. "But it' is too late to avoid permanent facial hair removal. You made a mistake and it cannot be taken back. I will arrange your appointment today and for your girlfriend, Candy." She loved to call them girlfriends and make them kiss passionately. "You will have laser hair removal. I cannot have any more slip-ups like last night."

Polly's eyes widened. He knew to say nothing.

"You are no longer a man, this procedure will be for the best. I will ask they laser your pubic hair into a pretty feminine triangle. Your girlfriend Candy will like that."

He looked down at the concrete floor of the car park. "Yes, Mistress, thank you," he replied with a soft sulky voice.

"Good girl." Aretta looked into his downcast eyes. Her work on him was not yet completed. Once she had arranged his breast implants, he should pass as a girl unless anyone looked too closely. His hands were a too large and wide, his shoulders were too broad. That was part of the fun for Aretta. She loved they retained some element of their past as this heaped humiliation on them.

Aretta hadn't yet told Polly about her plans for his breast implants. It was more amusing to find another pretend excuse, as she had with the laser treatment. She could do what she wanted with him but it was so much more fun to make them think it was their misbehaviour that led to more feminisation. A sort of petticoat punishment.

A thought came to her about how Polly never lost his vague male look. Her right cheek muscle tugged upwards in a grin as she had an idea. How he wouldn't pass as a girl due to his male facial look. She wondered why she had never thought of this before. Her face creased into a broad grin.

Chapter 4

The feminised journey

Aretta held out her hand as her smirk melted as she saw Polly did not understand what she wanted.

"I want the car keys," said Aretta.

Aretta watched his face wrinkle in alarm. He placed the keys in her open palm with rising panic. She chuckled inside.

"How will I get home, Mistress?" His voice wobbled.

"On the Metro train," came her blunt reply. She imagined him travelling home on public transport His tight mini skirt, bright blond hair and pink nails would attract looks. She loved the idea and wished she had the time to travel with him to see the attention.

His skirt was so short, his chastity cage and balls would show as soon as he sat down. If not before. She would travel with him another day to amuse herself, there was no time today.

She passed him a ten Euro note for the fare and marched to the executive lift. She pressed the call button and turned to see him standing with his mouth open in shock. The lift arrived and she left standing him in the car park. It whisked her to the executive top floor without stopping on any intermediate floors.

Aretta left the lift and marched towards her corner office. The fading image of Polly's anguished face rested in her mind. She chuckled.

Her private office was in the dicorner of the floor. It had glass walls on two sides with

Venetian blinds she could close for privacy. Outside the dark wooden polished door of her office, her personal secretary sat at a small reception desk. Her secretary was engrossed in reading from open light-blue plastic folder. Dark brown shoulder-length hair obscuring the face, slim hands curled long wavy hair in thin fingers.

"Good day, Carlos," said Aretta stopping in front of his desk.

His body jerked. A concerned look shot across his soft face before he replied. "Good day, Señora Ademola."

She smiled patronisingly on him. "Why do you always look so worried, little Carlos? I'm not going to bite?" She chuckled to herself before adding. "Yet."

His eyes widened in horror.

“Any messages, little Carlos?”

“Si señora, an agency called ExecLadies phoned. They didn't leave a message. They said it was personal. They are going to call back.”

Aretta had noticed an email from them on the way in. She hadn’t read it as she’d had to deal with other more pressing issues. She knew of the agency. ExecLadies was a prestigious organisation who headhunted senior female executives. Anticipation tingled through her. This seemed like good news.

Aretta's mind returned to the present. Her secretary was the only male secretary on the floor. The choice had been deliberate. “Follow me into my office, little Carlos.”

She swished into her office and sat behind a wide gloss-black desk. She settled into the high-backed black leather chair. This was her domain, her royal court. A closed laptop and a black telephone were the only items. On the desk-

Square two-seater black leather sofas sat at right angles to each other alongside. There was one on the external glass wall and the other on the internal wall. A small circular meeting table was positioned in front of it. Carlos stood in front of her desk, he fidgeted with his fingers and looked around.

Aretta leaned back in her chair. She had started to mould this young man to how she preferred men. She had requested a male secretary, they were more malleable and gave her some sport while she worked.

Carlos was perfect raw material. He was eager to please and with a thin small wiry body.

His thick hair and large brown eyes were a great base for what she had in mind for him. It had been easy to persuade him him, to let his hair grow. She had given him free access to her private hairdresser. He now had a pretty female hairstyle.

She had to be careful in her workplace to not be too open about her feminisation of Carlos. The changes had to be subtle, slow and to appear to be his decision. In some ways they were, he just needed a little persuasion.

This vulnerable young man was devoted to her. It was too tempting not to turn him into a girl. She couldn't help herself. His hairstyle was not subtle but his clothing was: female trousers and a white blouse with flat feminine shoes. Female clothing fitted his small frame well. He wasn’t obviously feminised but he didn’t look masculine either.

Many of Aretta’s colleagues had noticed Polly was not what *she* appeared to be at first glance. This was a source of amusement on the lower floors. Carlos’s changes had been spotted and many thought him gay. But Aretta knew he wasn't and knew he was besotted with her. This made this easier as she could do what she wanted. But all men became besotted with her.

Her few close friends knew about Aretta's proclivity for feminising males. Her close friends in the company were Marina Gonzalez, the company’s VP for Sales and her direct report and Silvia Belén, General Manager for Marketing. They had been to her apartment and enjoyed being served by the two maids. And impressed.

Caught up in her thoughts, Aretta realised Carlos was waiting for his orders.

"Little Carlos, I have three things for you. First, get me some coffee, I'm dying for caffeine. Two, set up the conference call with the web agency. Three, type up the notes from yesterday's marketing meeting." She trailed off as a thought entered her mind. Sport. "You look pretty today," she said.

Carlos blushed and dropped his head. He then did a wonderful thing, he bobbed down on a knee like a small curtsey knee. "Thank you, Señora Ademola."

She was getting through to his feminine and submissive side. She grinned to herself and added. "Your new trousers and blouse suit you, Carla." She slipped in the female version of his name to see how he reacted. It was time to up the ante.

Carlos's face dropped and his cheeks reddened. He didn't know what to say so she said nothing to exacerbate his discomfort. It was obvious he enjoyed his feminisation but needed a strong woman to push him. That was not going to be a problem.

"Thank you Señora Ademola, my new clothes are comfortable."

She noted he replied without admitting he liked them. She'd seen him stroking them in pleasure. "All the other secretaries wear skirts, Carla, maybe you would be more comfortable in a skirt, Carla? What do you think?"

She thought she saw him wobble, his legs unsteady. Was he was going to faint? She decided to press on, she was enjoying herself. She noted he'd said nothing about her calling him Carla.

"You can run along but think about my offer of wearing a skirt. I wouldn't mind. It would be lovely for you and everyone here, do you not think so? It must be difficult being the only male here. We can change that."

Carlos flushed bright red again. Aretta dismissed him with a wave of her hand. He breathed out a sigh of relief at the opportunity to escape. He stepped to the door.

Aretta called out. "Carla." She paused, seeing if he complained about the female name.

"Yes, Señora," he replied with a second sigh. He turned with a hand on the door handle as if it would allow him to escape.

"Think about my skirt offer and let me know." She smiled. "I will help select a pretty one for you."

His face dropped and his eyes popped in horror.

"Yes, thank you, Señora Ademola," he replied, a wobble in his throat.

"Thank you, *Carla*," Aretta answered back, emphasising the female version of his name again.

Carlos glanced at Aretta before closing the door. He ran to his desk. She chuckled again to herself, It was these little things that made life so enjoyable. She was close to getting Carlos into a skirt. She loved that moment in male feminisation. It was a turning point. The only thing holding her back in petticoating little

Carlos in one go was they were in her company offices. She had to do this gradually. That was fun too although Carlos was an easy challenge.

At that moment, the desk phone rang and broke her thoughts. She pressed the speaker key to answer. Carlos's nervous high voice greeted her with a metallic timbre from the small speaker.

"Señora, I have Ms Susan Tucci from ExecLadies on the line from London. She's the global CEO."

They are keen, she thought. The top dog herself. She knew exactly who Susan Tucci was. This must be serious.

Chapter 5

A New Chapter

“Put Ms Tucci through, Carla.” Aretta dropped in Carlos’s feminised name again. She smirked at the thought of him blushing deeply.

Susan Tucci was a regular in the business press and on the TV. Aretta would never have taken an unscheduled call from anyone who was not important. Or from a man.

The phone line clicked. “Hello, Aretta? Susan Tucci here, thank you so much for taking my unscheduled call.” Susan's strong New York accent greeted Aretta. Aretta had seen her on TV. She thought it would be good to meet her one day. She was sure from her style they shared a similar past-time.

“Nice to speak to you, Susan.” Aretta switched effortlessly from Spanish to British accented English. Two years of studies at the University of the City of London had honed her accent. She had taken a Masters’ degree in International Marketing. And passed in top place with distinction.

Susan Tucci got straight to the point. “I’m in London with a client. My client is the number one global marketing agency for female brands, FemFirst. They are looking for a new Global President of Marketing and they want to see you for an interview. To be honest they want you as they have dealt with you many times so the interview is a formality. They want to see you A-SAP.”

“OK,” said Aretta. “I’m listening.” Her tone

was was professional and calm. Inside, excitement mounted.

"They'll double your current salary, and give you a starting package which includes a share option scheme worth US$4 million. Also included would be free accommodation in central London. You have the opportunity to move to probably the most important marketing role anywhere in the world today for a woman. W*addaya think?*"

Aretta's brain whirled. She had made up her mind to take the job but didn't want to appear too enthusiastic while speaking to Susan Tucci.

"And what's the downside, Susan?" She asked injecting a hint of humour. She knew humour came across well. "There's always a downside, isn't there?"

"There is no downside, Aretta. You'd have to move to London as that's the agency's European headquarters."

Aretta delayed her reply. She wanted to make it seem she was considering what she had heard from Susan Tucci. In reality, she was enthusiastic about returning to London. The men were easy to control and feminise; she'd her own feminised maid when she lived there. By the time she had moved back to Madrid, she had even feminised four of her UCL classmates.

Her heart jumped a little. She was disappointed she realise she sometimes had emotions. In the circumstances, she would allow herself this excitement. It was a massive step up in her rise to the summit of achievement.

"I'll be happy to go to London for the

interview, Susan."

"Great, *Aredda,* I'll set it up," came Susan's reply.

"I'll wait for the details, Susan, thank you for your call."

Susan said *chao* and Aretta hung up with a sharp stab on the phone.

Aretta gazed out of the window. She gazed beyond the few skyscrapers of the business district and to the heart of the city. The tourist honeypot of Puerta del Sol stood out in the distance and beyond that, the old Grand Plaza.

Delight and exhilaration sparked like static on a telegraph pole in an electrical storm. She allowed her emotions to run for a few minutes. Normally she left her emotions in her private bedroom every morning.

A thought came to her mind, she'd need to move quickly with Carlos and to get him into a skirt before she left. She grinned to herself, it was always nice to have goals however small. And there was always time to feminise a male who needed a little push over the edge.

Chapter 6
His humiliation

Aretta's confidence was justified; she knew one day something better would come calling. And now it had. Having her employment contract clause of one month’s notice inserted was a master-stroke. She always planned for the next big thing.

Following her successful interview in London with Janet Walker, she was winding down her projects and handing over responsibilities.

Aretta breezed into her Madrid office, thankful for the chill of the air-conditioning. It was revving up to be a hot one in the city. There was one week before her move to London and a whole new place to dominate, business-wise and male-wise.

She breezed past Carlos, her mind elsewhere. She was considering how to complete her final marketing campaign for her current company. She wanted to leave on a high; those in the business would know.

She sat at her desk and turned on her laptop. As she was waiting for it to boot up, she felt someone staring at her. She looked to her right where the sensation came from. Through the open Venetian blinds, she spotted Carlos suddenly put his head down.

"Poor Carla, what will become of him without my guidance?" she thought, giving up any idea of using his male name.

An idea came to her. She was leaving the

company in good shape and, although she had resisted pushing his feminisation any further up to now, what harm would it do at this point? Her supreme expertise in business always gave her some leeway in her behaviour.

She continued to stare at Carlos as she thought about him as a pretty girl. He was almost there with his beautiful hair and pretty female blouses and trousers. Last week she had told him to shave his body hair and make sure he was always in panties under his trousers.

Carlos looked up, unsettled by her fixed gaze. She beckoned him with an index finger. She spotted a tremble of anticipation from him; he was besotted with her but also petrified by her.

Carlos rose from his chair with a dainty swish of his head. He went to her office. He knocked with a single knuckle. She called him in. He entered with his head bowed, his eyes on a space somewhere in front of her.

"Yes, Señora Ademola," he said. He brushed his thick hair away from his face in a feminine way. She noted how a male began to adopt feminine movements once she got them into female clothing and hairstyles.

Aretta walked around her desk and perched on the corner, one leg dangled. Aretta's tight dress rode up her leg revealing a dark toned leg. He looked away, avoiding eye contact like a puppy that had done something wrong. She had spotted Carlos's eyes dart to her exposed thigh and back away.

She didn't mind. His attraction for her made things simpler. "I hope you've continued to shave your body, Carla, and to wear pretty panties?" she said.

"Yes, Señora, of course," he mumbled.

She had never permitted him to waver from addressing her as Señora. She would have preferred Mistress but as they were in the company offices, señora would have to do.

"Show me your smooth legs, girly," she ordered with a raised eyebrow and crooked grin. She upped the ante by calling him a girly.

He looked around the room as if searching for an escape or a hole to fall through. Seeing his expression, she imagined he was thinking of others looking in. Aretta pressed a remote control button by her left hand. A soft faint mechanical whirring sounded and the blinds closed off the glass office from any outside gaze.

She slid the remote away across the polished surface of her desk. “We’re all alone now, Carla. I want you to drop your pretty trousers. I want to see your girly panties and smooth girly legs. I’m your boss for one more week so until then, you are *my* little girl.” She was pushing him harder but was comfortable with that. She doubted he would complain to HR.

Carlos squirmed and his hands fell across the front of his trousers.

“Come on, Carla,” purred Aretta. “I am waiting.” She adopted a sing-song tone she would have used with a child. “You do not want to keep me waiting. The consequences wil be worse.”

He stood frozen. He kept his hands across the front of his trousers as if they offered some barrier and protection. Aretta had to be a littler stricter; this girly-boy was timid. He needed direction.

Feminisation would be for the best for him, she was sure of that. It always was for males. She told him to stand in front of her. He moved close and stood, shaking a little. Aretta was unsure if it was in fear of her or anticipation of what was to come. Probably both.

"Let us see if you really are *little* Carla."

He winced at her implication.

She put out her right hand and flicked open the top button of his trousers. She jerked them down single-handed. They fell around his ankles, like collapsed sails on a windless sea.

He looked in shock. And in love. He breathed faster, his face and neck coloured into a deep shade of red. He licked his dry lips. His face showed a combination of pleasurable anticipation and horror.

She'd seen the look many times. Something about it told her he desperately wanted her to expose him. They all did, they just needed persuasion.

Aretta breathed in deeply, her body extended as if pulled to the ceiling by a winch. She was enjoying her power at the humiliation of little Carlos.

She put her mouth to his ear and whispered, "Step out of your trousers, Carla." Her lips brushed his ear, her rich perfume wafting around his nostrils.

He kicked his shoes away. She thought she could hear his heart pumping under his tight blouse. He was under her control. He kicked his trousers away and he stood in little white socks with a pink frill around the tops. She was pleased to see his legs were smooth. He had kept his legs very clear of hair, a good girly. He licked his dry lips again.

Aretta viewed him a few moments more before staring directly at the front of the silky pink panties. A twinkle came into her eyes as she thought about the next loss of dignity she was about to impose on him.

A jolt of electricity buzzed through her veins at her authority over feeble males. Carlos was her little pet allowing its Mistress to tickle its stomach. Carlos would allow her to have access to his vulnerability, ready to do whatever she decided. She loved that. Manipulation of a male was a gift.

He was aroused, evident by the tent that had formed in his silky panties. The small protrusion pointed at her. He looked at her with longing and desire, his mouth open, his eyelids drooping. She had him in the palm of her powerful hands. She could do anything she wanted with him. And she would, eventually, but not what he had in his private dreams. He wanted love from her but he was about to get humiliation.

"I can see you are excited, little Carla."

He let out a short high pitched whine from a dry throat. Aretta smelled his longing. His delight and love of her invasion of his intimate privacy.

"You are *little*." She sniggered while staring at the tent in his panties.

The first look of doubt appeared on his face. She smiled kindly and he relaxed slightly. She got up and went over to the office door and flicked the key to lock it. His body tensed again.

"We do not want anyone to disturb us, do we girly? You do not want others to see just how tiny you are down there, do you?"

Carlos shook his head. Aretta stood and towered over his slight frame. She grabbed his erection through his panties and squeezed hard, digging her dark red nails in. She let go and he jumped at the surprise, letting out a muffled gargle.

He asked, "Señora?"

"Relax," she said, returning to her perch on the corner of the desk. She looked again at the protrusion in his panties.

"You have a tiny willy," she cooed.

"Señora?" he repeated.

"I said you have a tiny willy."

"Señora, maybe I should get dressed now." His discomfort at her verbal humiliation of his manhood had raised the first doubts. His body turned towards the door.

"In time Carla, in time. First, I want you to show me what you have hiding in those pretty panties. Not much."

He lost the look of a puppy dog to be replaced by one of disquiet and apprehension.

"Show me your dick, girly, I do not want to have to ask again." Aretta's sweet demeanour faded.

Carlos was a good boy but Aretta could only put up with so much. Seeing her face darken,

Carlos knew he had to do as she ordered. He had no choice. The atmosphere in the office had chilled even though the sun was streaking through the gaps in the closed blinds.

Aretta grew bored of his dithering and hooked two fingers into the top of his panties and ripped them down. Carlos gasped as his little erect penis bounced free, exposed to her stern gaze.

"Much better, *little* Carla." She was enjoying herself again, her face softened.

She grabbed his erection with a finger and thumb and pulled him close, the skin at its base was taut and stretched. Tears welled in his eyes at the humiliation and of the joy of her touching him.

"What a very tiny little thing you have, Carla.

This is more like a little girl's clitty, is it not? I was right, you are a girl." Her smirk returned as she kept hold of his little erection, holding it and rolling it between her finger and thumb like a cigarette. Her face was set in mock disdain.

Carlos stared at her fingers as they played with his erect penis. She saw his discomfort with disguised pleasure. The trouble was, he was not a challenge. This was too easy. Like a sugar rush and then nothing.

She stood up and let go of his erection. She went back to sit behind her desk, leaving Carlos standing. She saw he didn't know what to do. Good, that was fun when they felt that way. She started typing emails as if he wasn't there, as if she had forgotten him.

"Señora, what should I do?" he said in a thin

voice.

She continued typing, peering into her screen. “One moment, Carla, I have to deal with this email first.”

Carlos waited. He was perplexed as he looked down at his hard erection pulsing. She guessed he was desperate to cum.

“Right,” said Aretta suddenly and she glanced up without interest. “Milk yourself to get rid of your nasty little erection. Then you will get back to work. I have too much to do to continue playing with you so get on with it and then leave me.”

Carlos gasped, “Excuse me, Señora?”

“You heard,” she snapped back. “Milk yourself and get out.”

She fished in her handbag giving out a loud

sigh of frustration. She pulled out a pack of tissues. She slid them across the desk towards him and they fell off the end and onto the floor.

"Use these to catch your nasty mess, I do not want it on my floor. Wipe yourself clean after. I do not want to find any drips on the carpet."

Carlos picked up the tissue pack, his stiff penis wiggled from side to side as he shuffled. Aretta remained engrossed in her emails. She was impassive but inside her emotions were ecstatic. She continued to pretend to work while she watched him from the corner of her eye. He started to pump his little penis at a tissue.

His face grimaced and he was staring at her as he masturbated. She imagined she was the object of his masturbation fantasies.

"Hurry. Get it over with, girly." Her face

remained glued to the screen, apparently disinterested.

From her peripheral vision saw him rubbing more rapidly, then he muttered an, "Argh," and jerked as his cum shot into the tissue. She fought the need to smile broadly.

"Are you done?" she asked coolly.

"Yes, Señora," came the weak response as he continued to have after spasms. "Thank you."

"Clean up, get dressed and get out."

"Yes, Señora," he replied as he wiped his flaccid penis dry.

She was unable to stop herself smiling. He had even thanked her for allowing him to play with his little thing. He dressed and made his way to her office door, still holding the tissue.

"Carla," she called as he opened the door.

He looked around at her, worry etched on his face.

"Bring in the air freshener to spray around in here. I do not want to work under the odour of your cum."

"Yes, Señora."

"I will bring a pretty skirt for you to wear tomorrow. It is no longer right for you to wear trousers."

She looked down again and ignored him. He looked at her for a moment and then shook his head and closed her door and scurried to his desk, petrified and electrified.

Chapter 7

The Feminisation of Carlos

There were only four days to go until Aretta's left for her new life in London. She allowed herself a small grin at Carlos's face when she told him she was going to put him in a skirt today.

Her ears popped as the ping of the lift indicated she had arrived at the top floor. The doors slid open with a swish. She hesitated a moment to ensure she had her body upright, her head straight and her pose right. Appearances were important even if she was leaving.

She stepped out into the office and wondered if Carlos would show up today. After her promise to put him in a skirt today, he might be too worried.

She had enjoyed humiliating Carlos yesterday it gave her a sharp tingle. Even though he was an easy target, she loved the devotion he showed her. She had the power to do as she pleased with him. That was a good thing.

She saw he was at his desk. He was on the phone. She heard his high-pitched voice explaining that Señora Ademola wasn't available but he would check her diary and get back to them. Game on.

She stopped by his desk and looked down on him. Her handbag was slung over her shoulder and she carried a leather holdall. She held it up to show him.

“What do you think I have in here, Carla?”

His eyes widened in alarm and he shook his head. He didn't believe she’d carry out her threat.

He’ll learn. She decided not to admonish him for not greeting her correctly; she had more important things in mind today.

“Today is the day I put you in a skirt, Carla. It is in here for you to put on later, as I promised.” She shook the bag in front of him with pleasure.

She eyed him up and down seeing he seemed to accept his fate. He replied in a cowed manner, “OK, Señora,” before looking away, trying to avoid eye contact. He wanted this, she thought.

Aretta entered her office as a low morning orange sun speared into the room. She closed the blinds to avoid the glare. She wouldn't have so much sun in London, she reflected.

She had completed her remaining tasks; she had set aside these final four days for preparation for her new job in London. And new fun. The new job would be more demanding but she was more than ready to make it a success. Nevertheless, she never took anything for granted and would work hard and diligently as always. It was the only route to success.

She glanced at her watch, it was nearly 8.30 am. She'd arranged to meet her friend, Marina Gonzalez from Sales that evening in her office. She had not yet told Carlos as she had something interesting in mind for him.

Marina had the most efficient secretary in the company: Dolores, a fearsome middle-aged lady. Dolores had been married many years ago but divorced a couple of years ago. Many said she wore her husband out by her demands. Despite her best attempts at finding romance on internet sites, she never had success.

Marina believed Dolores was too fearsome for most men and too keen and desperate. This frightened men away. Her dress front was too low, her hem too short, her perfume too strong and her clothing too obvious and young for a woman her age. Aretta had said Dolores sounded perfect for what she had in mind for Carlos that evening.

Aretta picked up the phone and called Carlos. "You will stay behind tonight as I am having a small leaving event in my office with two friends. I want you to attend."

He accepted without enthusiasm but she knew he would be there. She had commanded it.

The day passed quickly. Carlos appeared to forget about Aretta's promise to petticoat him or at least thought her threat was an empty one. By evening, Carlos was alone in the open office and Aretta had shut herself away in her office with the blinds down. Apart from when she asked for coffee or a sandwich at lunchtime, communication and contact with her had been sparse.

By late afternoon, Carlos had finished his work and was killing time until the leaving event. The lift pinged, announcing the arrival of Aretta's two guests for the farewell event. Marina strode out, the epitome of a power-dressed corporate woman. Dolores followed behind her. Dolores frightened Carlos, she was abrupt and, at times, plain rude.

"Aretta's expecting us," Marina said as she breezed by Carlos and into Aretta's office without breaking stride. Dolores ambled behind her and glanced at Carlos before closing the door behind her.

Aretta got up from her desk and walked round to kiss Marina on both cheeks. She raised a palm in greeting to Dolores. Aretta had told Carlos to bring in the bottle of red wine once they arrived. He brought the wine in with four glasses. He opened it and poured it into four glasses. He served them to each of the women. Marina took hers and noticed for the first time his female trousers and blouse.

"Well, aren't you the pretty one?" she exclaimed. "And your hairstyle. Pretty." She looked back to Aretta. "You've done well with him. Or should that be her?"

"Are you him or her, Carla?" Aretta asked

him.

He cowered in humiliation.

"How wonderful, you've given him a girl's name," Marina beamed.

Dolores looked on impassively weighing up the situation.

Aretta, still looking at Marina, said, "I have brought a skirt in for her to put on, shall we have a fashion show, ladies?"

Carlos now realised Aretta forgot nothing after all. As if to prove it, Aretta rummaged through the leather bag she had waved in front of Carlos earlier in the day. She pulled out a short grey skirt with front box pleats. "The schoolgirl look," she announced.

Carlos put his hands to his mouth.

"Oh yes, Aretta, I think that would be

wonderful.” Marina turned to address Carlos. “Put the pretty skirt on, Carla,”

Aretta passed the skirt to him. He took with a petulant snatch. Aretta guessed he had hoped it would be just her and him. An audience was more fun.

“Do not be a naughty girl or I will have to spank in front of these ladies. You would not want that, would you? Or maybe you would?” Aretta looked at him with a hint of fire in her eyes.

Carlos couldn’t speak. Aretta turned away from him and started speaking to Marina and Dolores.

“Yesterday, she got her little willy out for me here in the office and made a mess into a tissue. I thought she was looking desperate so I let her play with herself." Aretta recounted the story from yesterday as Marina laughed. Dolores's eyes lit up. She could smell the blood of a vulnerable man.

"Come on, Carla, put the skirt on," Dolores now joined in.

The three ladies turned, Aretta with her hands on her hips waiting for Carlos. He brushed a long lock of hair from his eyes, no more than a minor delaying tactic. Aretta was confident he wanted this. This moment that would change him forever. Putting a male into a skirt, specially a humiliating schoolgirl skirt, was a defining moment. Delicious.

Chapter 8

A boy's new skirt

"Dolores, help her remove her trousers," said Aretta.

Dolores reacted faster than Carlos expected. While he was still digesting what she'd said, Dolores was on him. Her hands were on his trousers, tugging them off. She kneeled, following them down. She told him to step out of them as he held on to his panties which had almost came down with the trousers.

Carlos complied with a sulk, he had no option, it was three against one. They had this planned and he had nowhere to run. Dolores knelt to inspect his erect cock poking out in the front of his pink panties. She hesitated and looked back at Aretta. "It's tiny, as you said Aretta."

Dolores pulled the front of his panties out and peeked inside at his erect penis. The two friends, Aretta and Marina, sipped on their wine and sat to watch events unfold.

"I told you Dolores would like this," said Marina between sips of wine.

Dolores slid Carlos's panties down and pulled them out from under his feet. He stood exposed and agitated. His small erection was firm and erect, his head fell down. Dolores took the skirt and pulled it up his legs and adjusted it around his waist. She stood and stepped back.

Carlos breathed a sigh of relief. He was covered again and away from Dolores's leering stare.

“Beautiful,” said Marina. “She’s better as a girl. I can’t believe you turned little Carlos into a pretty girl.”

Aretta looked into her bag again and pulled out a pair of brown shoes with a small heel. “Put these on, Carla. Your flat shoes may be female but they are not female enough. You need a heel to make your legs look prettier.”

Carlos put the shoes on and walked unsteadily. He was unused to the heels.

“Carla, serve us some more more,” ordered Aretta. Carlos left Aretta’s office, walking with care in his new shoes and heels. The grey pleated cotton skirt swayed as he went to the kitchen area where Aretta had left the other bottle of wine. The women watched through the open door. He returned.

“With makeup and boobs, she would pass as a girl without any problem,” said Marina.

“Maybe that could be your job once I’ve left, Marina,” replied Aretta.

“Can I have her?” Dolores interjected and Aretta and Marina stopped talking and thought.

Together they smiled and agreed “Yes, why not?”

Carlos looked confused, “Have me?”

They ignored him and they chatted together after sitting on the black sofas in the office. Carlos remained standing in the middle of the room. His short grey pleated skirt remained pushed out at the front by his erection.

Can I play with her now, Marina?” asked Dolores.

“Go ahead,” answered Marina.

Carlos didn't understand what they meant and backed away until he hit against Aretta's desk. Dolores sauntered over to him, a craving and lustful expression across her face. He cowered as her eyes narrowed and her shoulders dropped as if she were ready to pounce. She was.

She moved into his personal space. Aretta and Marina leant back on the sofa, side by side, their long lean legs crossed in mirror images of each other. They prepared to watch the show. It was about to start.

Dolores reached to the hem of his skirt and lifted it. Carlos put his hands on the desk, looking for some support. Her eyes remained fixed on his. Her irises expanded and her eyes sparked. She grabbed at his penis. She took it with index finger and thumb. He looked to

Aretta, his mouth opened and closed, his eyes crying help. No help was coming. This was the show.

Dolores squeezed his penis hard between her fingers. She let go and put both her hands on the front of his skirt holding it up to his stomach. Carlos whined in embarrassment.

She knelt so her eyes were level with his erection. Carlos looked back and forth again to Aretta and Marina. They watched as if they were at the theatre watching a show.

Dolores's dark curly hair was streaked with slices of grey. Her head moved forward towards his erection. Her lips opened a little and she planted them on the end of his erect head. She poked her tongue out and explored the slit at the end.

Carlos shivered with horror and delight. Dolores's lips slid over the swollen head but no further. She moved back, leaving then on the very end in a pursed up shape. Her tongue brushed the end again

She opened her mouth wider and moved over his small erection and all the way to his balls. She sucked hard with a single slurp.

Marina called out, "Can you feel him, Dolores, he's so tiny."

Dolores nodded with his small erection still inside her mouth. Aretta and Marina giggled at this.

Dolores withdrew one of her hands from his skirt and it fell onto her head. She slipped her hand around to his bum cheek while she sucked on his penis harder. She moved her mouth back and forward in a regular motion.

Carlos moaned, forgetting he was the show. He closed his eyes. Aretta told Marina he was now enjoying it and that made her happy. He opened his eyes. Dolores kept her mouth and tongue motion going. She turned Carlos side on so their audience could see better.

She moved her hand up his bottom cheek until her middle finger touched the ring of his bottom. She scratched at it, causing him to flinch with surprise. Her finger then thrust up inside him. He jerked, face in shock.

She wiggled her finger and kept it deep inside him. Carlos closed his eyes again. Aretta saw he was loving this humiliation. She had guessed correctly, Carlos was prime sissy material.

Carlos froze. He was about to cum. Dolores felt it too. She whipped out her finger and took her mouth away from his penis. She moved to one side just in time. He didn't cum, she'd taken her finger and mouth away at the crucial moment.

"I don't want your nasty stuff in my mouth," Dolores looked up at him. She raised herself and went to sit on the other sofa.

"Do we leave her desperate or shall we let her masturbate herself?" said Marina.

"Don't be cruel," laughed Aretta. She tapped her friend playfully on the arm.

"Your boss is too kind, Carla, I wouldn't allow it. You can jerk yourself off but catch it in something," Marina said.

Dolores stood and passed Carlos an empty

wine glass. “Jack off into the glass, girly,” she ordered.

The women laughed.

Carlos took the glass with desperation. He pushed his erection inside the rim and waited.

“Get on with I, I want to go home,” said Aretta.

He put his hand to his penis and rubbed. He watched Aretta and rubbed faster. Aretta frowned, looking at her watch.

“Aretta, she’s watching you while she does it,” Marina yelled. “She’s using you as her fantasy.”

He came. A warm glow fell over his face as the first shot of his thick juices hit the bottom of the glass. Dolores clapped and beamed with delight.

Carlos finished cumming and immediately his face registered shock. He stood with his limp cock hanging into a wine glass full of semen. It dripped to the gooey mess.

Marina stood up and announced, “Time to go, show over and very interesting it was too. Nice work Aretta.”

“Thank you for coming, ladies, you too, Carla – in both senses.” Aretta sneered at him.

“Don’t forget to drink it all up, Carla,” said Marina

“Drink it up then we can go,” Aretta repeated.

Carlos let his skirt drop and looked down at the partly filled glass, the salty odour rose from the wine glass. They saw he didn’t find the prospect attractive. He looked up and the three ladies were waiting. Aretta walked over and slapped him on the face.

"Drink it, girly. In time, if Marina has her way, you'll be drinking plenty of this. And it won't be yours."

He put the glass to his lips. He closed his eyes and retched. He threw the contents down his throat and retched again.

"You know girls have to swallow." Marina walked to the door and spun around. "She looks cute in her skirt. She should go home in it."

"A great idea, she may as well get used to it," replied Aretta.

Carlos looked aghast as Aretta took his trousers and stuffed them into her leather bag. She paused and looked at the floor, lost in thought.

“What are you thinking, Aretta?” Marina asked seeing her friend pensive for the first time that evening.

“Yes, I'm fine. I was thinking how I’m going to have to find a new maid when I get to London. What fun. Half the fun is the training.”

“Yes,” replied Marina. “Look out Englishmen, Aretta’s coming for you. Again.”

Part 2

Stephen's Story

Chapter 9

The interview

The Victorian building was five stories of yellow brick. It had a garden pub and restaurant on the flat roof. Stephen had never been to this gentrifying and developing area before. When he was young, it used to be an inner-city slum.

The tall sash windows of this former clothing factory reflected the clouds passing above. The sandblasted yellow brick walls were formed from the local clay. A watery morning sun peeked out intermittently through low dark clouds. A sharp autumn breeze rustled the green and brown leaves of the silver birches planted in the verges of this cul-de-sac. Summer was coming to an end.

The roar of crawling vehicles from the High Street assaulted Stephen Hayley's ears as walked along the road. He made his way to a former factory site, now a small industrial estate for high tech, product design and marketing companies.

He turned into the industrial zone. He'd made it to a second interview; this was his big opportunity. He walked to the old factory unit and hesitated at the entrance. He took a deep breath to compose himself. A taste of autumn air flowed to his lungs with an after-taste of diesel.

His short greying hair suited his lean face and tall slim physique. He was comfortable to be in a business suit again.

He had been Head of Marketing only twelve months ago but not now. The Managing Director of his previous company had a shock for him:

they were making him redundant. At the age of fifty-one, he knew finding a job as good as the one he had been in was going to be difficult. It had proved impossible. Companies today wanted keen young highly educated young people on lower salaries.

His redundancy money was running low and Stephen and his wife Rebecca were moving inexorably into debt. He had a mortgage and a bank loan. They had moved up to a larger house and a bigger car thinking the job would be forever. Rebecca had pointed out it was risky at their age but he had been confident. That confidence was misplaced and the bank was losing patience. Threatening letters had begun to arrive. He needed this job, any job.

It wasn't just the money, being unemployed

had been an enormous blow to his male pride and ego. He’d always provided for Rebecca. She had a good job as a primary school teacher but it didn't pay anything like his old job. Besides, he was old-fashioned; he felt it was his role as the man to ensure they lived well.

Rebecca had always supported him in this. With a senior well-paid role, life had been wonderful. It wasn’t now. Rebecca told him she could see his body beginning to sag, his erect stature and confidence had evaporated. It had disappeared with the job. He always thought he was capable of anything but now he didn’t know. He felt useless, supported by his wife and the Government with a meagre unemployment allowance.

How demeaning, queuing in the

employment agency with young people in their baseball caps, trainers and polyester tracksuits. All that to receive a weekly amount he'd earn in an hour when he was Head of Marketing.

Rebecca had found the job advert, placed in a magazine aimed at women. The company was a globally-renown marketing agency with a focus on women's products. The role was for a Marketing Assistant. He had argued with his wife he was a senior manager. Rebecca pointed out he wasn't, he was an unemployed ex-senior manager with no income.

Rebecca pushed Stephen to apply, he possessed all the qualifications and experience they asked for and more. Except for one thing: knowledge and experience of the female marketplace. He didn't think he was what they wanted; he was male, middle-aged and his years were starting to show. He couldn't argue with Rebecca, she was right. They needed the salary so he applied and he got an interview.

It had been a tough first interview with the European Managing Director, Janet Walker, and Aretta Ademola, the Global President of Marketing. They were an impressive couple for an interview for the junior position of Marketing Assistant.

He knew he had done well enough but he wondered if, as a man, they would choose him. Yet here he was, standing outside their offices for a second interview. Yesterday he had received a phone call from Ms Walker's PA to tell him they had been impressed with his performance in the interview. They wanted to see him again for the second interview.

"It looks like being female wasn't so necessary after all," Rebecca had told him. She was usually right, thought Stephen, still composing himself at the entrance.

Ms Walker's PA had added that Ms Walker had concerns over his lack of experience in the female market. Ms Walker, and the new Marketing President, wanted to discuss this. If it went well, they had a proposal to make things work out. She didn't want to elaborate over the phone.

Stephen looked at his watch, 9.55 am, five minutes to the interview, it was time to go in.

He entered the reception area through a glass door that didn't match the Victorian exterior. He felt the fresh artificial atmosphere of office air-conditioning. He walked to the high-fronted teak-coloured reception desk. A young lady was sitting behind the counter.

The clacking of her long nails sounded against the keys of a keyboard hidden below the high reception desk. Busy with her typing, she hadn't noticed him and didn't look up.

He coughed politely and announced, "I'm here to see Janet Walker and Aretta Ademola. My name is Stephen Hayley."

She looked up and pulled a practised smile. Above her head, a large sign displayed the company name followed by a slogan in smaller text:

'FemFirst: Marketing for Females by Females'

Maybe by males now, he thought.

"Hello Mr Hayley, they are expecting you. I'll show you to the meeting room."

She walked around her desk and past an entrance to the main office protected by a swipe-card security box. and then past a single lift opposite the reception desk. She showed him over to a door in the corner of the area labelled *meeting room*. She swung open the door and stood back, holding with an extended arm. Stephen slipped past her and into the room.

She asked him to take a seat and wait for Ms Walker and Ms Ademola.

He looked around. It was more of a holding area than a meeting room. He'd had the first interview here and hadn't been in the main office or seen the operation during his previous time there. He remained standing and looked around, tapping his fingers on the circular light oak conference table. It had four seats arranged around it.

A black conference phone shaped like a menacing crab sat in the centre of the table. A large shiny-leafed fig tree was in a dull silver pot. It was squeezed in the corner making it difficult to walk around the room. Black and white photos of models in dresses and arty shots of well-known products hung from the walls. Spotlights in the ceiling threw a stark white light over everything.

Stephen wandered to a metal barred window that looked out onto a foot-way leading back to the high street. He saw a mix of passers-by striding to their jobs. Some were young and trendy; they looked like product designers or IT workers. These industries had shot up here in the past few years. The area was regenerating in a district that had once housed the garment industries of an earlier period

The door swished open and Janet Walker entered the room followed by the tall slim athletic Aretta Ademola. She was as dark and brooding before. She made him uncomfortable.

Stephen swallowed hard, his mouth dry. He had a second interview, he was in with a chance. But the role was junior, what did they want from him?

Chapter 10

Coming to the point

They sat opposite him.

He guessed Janet Walker to be around fifty. Her light blond hair was dead straight with a curl up at the ends. The curl bounced against her shoulders as she walked. Her fringe hung to her well-defined eyebrows.

She wore a slim sleeveless white dress, an inch above her knee. She had a pearl necklace around her neck that gave an air of affluence to her dignified manner. Her slim arms and legs hinted at a body that spent hours in a gym.

Around her eyes, the skin was crease-less, Stephen guessed it had seen a fair amount of Botox or surgery. She was straight-backed with a striding walk. She had a pleasant half-smile on her lips and kindness around her eyes. She was comfortable and familiar with being in charge

Aretta Ademola was a different proposition. Her BBC-styled accent sounded artificial and practised. Rebecca had looked her up online and seen she was brought up in Nigeria and Spain; English was not her first language.

Aretta was also confident and assertive but unlike Ms Walker, there was no warmth. There was something else in her eyes and her expression; something behind her mask of impassiveness he couldn't read.

He was overwhelmed with Aretta's magnetism, her beauty and her poise. She possessed a power that oozed from every part of her body. He never doubted his devotion to

Rebecca but Aretta had something he had never encountered before. It was a feeling she could entice him in and do anything she wanted. The feeling was frightening and exhilarating.

If he were to be successful today in this second interview, Aretta would be his boss. This would be challenging in many ways. A thrill engulfed him he couldn't explain. She was fierce. He shuddered at the prospect.

“Thank you for coming back to see us. dear,” Janet Walker’s smile creased her eyes and mouth. Her impeccable diction suggested she had benefited from a private exclusive education.

“We were impressed with you in the first interview,” she continued, furrowing her eyebrows and lowering her head. “However, we have a snag. FemFirst’s policy is to employ only those who understand the female market. This, of course, means women." She lowered her eyes. "That fact does not go outside this room."

Stephen shook his head. He understood from his previous role, employment law does not allow recruitment based on gender. He also understood there were many ways companies found ways around this.

Janet Walker spotted his vacant look as he pondered their women-only policy. "We didn't expect to get an application from a male due to our advertising channels. Nevertheless, we were keen we give you a try as your CV was most impressive. To be more accurate, Aretta wanted to give you the chance and suggested a male might give us a new perspective." She glanced at Aretta for a moment.

"You were head and shoulders above anyone else in the first interview. You seem also to be a sensitive person, which we liked. Aretta said you could almost be a female with your sensitivity." She giggled girlishly. "This made us chuckle,"

Janet Walker chuckled again and allowed herself a moment's reflection at the incident. Aretta stared hard at him. He looked away and tried to ignore her. He felt her gaze burning into him. So far, Aretta had said nothing but he knew she was analysing him.

"We need, therefore, to cover some additional areas with you and gain some confidence before we can offer the position. If all this proves to be OK for us, and to you, we will make an offer. How does that sound, dear?"

Stephen sat up. He felt a buzz of anticipation.

It was a junior position but work was work and he was desperate. “I’m pleased you liked my interview and I’m sure I can provide you with the confidence to employ me. I’m flexible and willing to fit in with whatever you propose,” Stephen replied.

Aretta who was watching him with her fixed unblinking deep blue eyes and a stern expression. He felt a tingle of anticipation at her attention. He couldn’t push it away entirely.

“I’m glad you feel that way, dear,” said Janet Walker, oblivious to his discomfort at Aretta’s attention. “This is the attitude we are looking for. We would expecting a high degree of flexibility from you. Of course, the role is far more junior than your previous role and will include office administration duties. You understand, don’t you? You will be the most junior person here."

Stephen noticed she said 'will' and not the conditional 'would'. A pulse of excitement ran through him, they wanted him. His mind raced onto how pleased Rebecca would be, how proud of him she would be.

He swallowed to compose himself. "I understand, Ms Walker and Ms Ademola, and I have no problem with that. I'm looking forward to working again, if you decide to choose me." His eyes flitted briefly to Aretta. Goodness, she was imposing and stunning. She was distracting him.

The phone on the conference table rang and Aretta picked it up. "Yes, I will him to collect them," she said into the phone. She looked across at Stephen. "Our receptionist has made coffee for but cannot leave the reception desk. Be a good boy and collect the drinks and bring them back here." She put the phone down.

He saw she expected him to comply without question. Stephen leaned back in his chair. Good boy? "You want me to collect the coffee, Ms Ademola?"

"That is what I said, was it not?" She didn't look up. "Janet and need a private chat about you and this role." She looked up and glared. "I assume this is not a problem?"

That made sense although calling him good boy was demeaning. He had little choice, he had to show his willingness. This was a junior role so he would have to get used to this. "Of course, no problem, Ms Ademola." He smiled thinly. She hadn't asked, she had ordered, he thought.

He raised himself with studied reluctance from the chair. He trudged out of the meeting room to reception. Three cups of coffee waited on the counter of the reception desk.

This is going to be difficult, he thought. He shrugged. Aretta was an oddball. He walked back into the meeting room and placed the drinks in front of the two ladies. He picked up one for himself. They ignored him and carried on speaking between themselves for a couple of minutes about someone called Anne.

It was obvious the two ladies had a good relationship although, he knew from Rebecca's online search, Aretta had only joined the agency a couple of weeks previously.

Aretta leaned forward and, without preamble, asked him a few questions on specific

Marketing areas. They were straightforward questions and she seemed satisfied with his answers.

Aretta wrote a note and asked without looking up, “How do you feel about working only with women?”

Stephen replied, “I have always preferred the company of women. I enjoy an occasional afternoon at football with my male friends but I socialise with women.” He had two good platonic female friends and was also happy to spend an evening with Rebecca and her girlfriends.

“I’m comfortable with the prospect of working in a female environment and, in all truth, I’d say I prefer the idea.”

Aretta’s glare seemed to spear into his mind. He had never seen a lady with such dark skin and piercing blue eyes. They were enticing and sexy but as cold as ice.

"At least 30 to 40% of this role is administration," Aretta said, snapping him from his thoughts. "This includes running errands, photocopying, preparing presentations for me, taking minutes and duties like that. It will mean bringing coffee for me, as you've just done successfully with no problems." She smiled thinly, her brilliant white perfect teeth glinted in the morning sunlight from the windows.

He pondered her point, ruefully recalling how far he had fallen; from Head of Marketing to coffee-making assistant. "Yes, Ms Ademola, I understand." He did not want to do administration tasks but this was all he had. He needed to think of Rebecca.

"Excellent," said Ms Walker. "You have shown us you have the ability to understand what motivates women and you show more sensitivity than most men I know. Aretta is impressed too which is always difficult. She has high standards. However, you are not a woman and this remains a problem for us."

"Yes, Ms Walker, but I am sure I can learn that aspect of the role," said Stephen. "If I have any questions, I can always ask my wife."

"No," Ms Walker interrupted. "I'm afraid that's not enough, dearie."

"I'm sorry," answered Stephen, not knowing what he was apologising for. He thought it best to show some contrition all the same.

Aretta watched him with a leer, like a lioness surveying its prey.

Ms Walker continued. “The post comes with an excellent salary for such a junior role. There are five weeks’ holiday and health insurance for you and your spouse. But.”

She hesitated to allow her ‘*but*’ to sink in. “Before we make an offer, you need to accept the proposal we’re about to make. Your acceptance must be complete and without reservation. This proposal will help to get over the problem of you not being female.”

Ms Walker sat back and allowed a small grin to come onto her lips. “It was Aretta’s idea and, whilst unusual, it is inventive. I hope you accept it.”

Chapter 11

The proposal

Ms Walker leaned forward. “I will let Aretta explain our proposal. Before she does, I have to state our proposal is quite unusual. We will not put it into writing. If you accept it, you will to sign a contractual document to state it was all your idea. Our lawyer has drafted this letter in anticipation. No one outside of this room will know of our agreement, even the lawyer believes she drafted it at your request.”

“I can’t imagine there will any problem, Ms Walker. I’m keen to start work here.” That wasn’t strictly true but he needed work and was keen for the income.

”Excellent,” said Ms Walker. She turned to

her companion. “Aretta?”

A small smile appeared on the corner of Aretta’s lips. He shivered at her gaze.

“Our proposal is not negotiable,” said Aretta. “You must accept it in full without amendment. Do you understand me?”

“Yes, absolutely,” said Stephen, trying to sound enthusiastic. “I’m willing to work long hours and take on any task,” he added.

“That is nice but not what I mean. Our proposal is this.” She waited for him to concentrate. “Whenever you are in this office, you will use only the products we market for our customers. Do you understand what this means?”

“Yes, of course. I’ll use the products you market. I see no problem,” said Stephen, wondering what her point was.

Aretta looked annoyed. “I am not convinced you understand. We market only female products so you can only use female products.”

Stephen frowned and nodded to himself. He contemplated Aretta’s proposal. He was unsure where this was going and what products she was talking about. Aretta was waiting for his reply.

“I’m sure I can find some of the products you market that would be suitable to use even though they are for women.”

Aretta’s mouth tightened and she glanced up at the ceiling. She tapped her nails on the tabletop a couple of times. Ms Walker sat back without comment, observing Stephen’s reaction with interest.

Aretta stopped tapping. “We market female

perfume, makeup and....” She stared straight at him, her small smile disappearing. “Female clothes. Nothing you wear in our offices can be male. Nothing.”

Stephen glanced at Ms Walker and saw no reaction. She had a single raised eyebrow. She was waiting for his response.

Aretta continued. “You will wear female clothes at all times at work. Everything we wear and use in the office are the products we market for our clients. It's company policy and we trade on this policy.”

Stephen fidgeted from side to side in his chair. Suddenly, he felt very uncomfortable. He tugged at his collar with a single finger. His eyes darted from Aretta to Ms Walker then back. Both were looking at him without expression, waiting, gauging his reaction.

"You want me to wear female clothes?" Stephen said softly. He was uncertain how to react. This was not what he had expected but he didn't want to jeopardise his opportunity to get a job. He wasn't going to wear a dress, that much was sure. He'd tell them to stick their job if that's what they wanted.

Aretta spoke. "You will wear female moisturiser and perfume. You need to feel feminine to market femininity. You see my point?"

This sounded reasonable. But a skirt? A dress? No way. That was not happening. He breathed in slowly and deeply. He licked his dry lips. He felt confused and warm. He chewed on his bottom lip and looked at his hands held flat on the table.

Ms Walker and Aretta shared a glance. He was frozen. What to do? In his preparation for the interview, he had not considered there would be such an unusual proposal. He wasn't prepared.

Ms Walker spoke. "I realise this is a surprise. We would love to have you with us at FemFirst but you need to accept our proposal." Ms Walker spoke with a soft compassionate voice, her head inclined to one side to make her point.

Aretta spoke next. "We will provide all the *female* products free of charge. We will provide uni-sex styles, such as dark business suits, white blouses and so on. I am certain this approach will work and no one will even notice. You would change here in the meeting room before entering the office. You can arrive in your male clothing.

However, I reiterate. Everything you wear once you enter the FemFirst office beyond the security doors will be from our female-only ranges."

Ms Walker smiled. "We are making a massive concession for you to demonstrate how much we want you to join us. We have a no-trousers policy but we will waive this for you. If you meet us halfway. So, Stephen. What is your answer? We have made you a straightforward proposal and we need a straightforward response from you. And you must give your answer now as we will need to find an alternative urgently if you decline our generous offer."

Stephen's face and neck flushed red. "May I phone my wife?" This was a delaying tactic to get his mind together as he thought about their proposal. It was not meeting halfway, more like meeting 90% in their favour.

"No," said Aretta. "You must decide now. We have other candidates. You must decide now."

Aretta was becoming impatient. Ms Walker nodded her agreement.

"Your answer?" said Aretta

His mind raced with options. He pondered how might get away with this. When they find how good he is, wearing female products may not seem so important. He deliberated on how desperate he was for money. And how desperate he was for Rebecca's respect again. Rebecca had wanted him to go for this job, it was her who had pushed him to apply. He wanted to buy time but there was none. He supposed he could resign if it didn't work so why not give it a go? He had to answer. Now.

"OK," he sighed, "I accept your proposal. I think with neutral female clothes, it may work." He was unconvinced but tried to sound positive. And he could tell them he wasn't coming if he changed his mind or Rebecca was unhappy at the idea.

"Excellent," said Ms Walker clasping her hands together. "Aretta will arrange all details with you and get you measured up. You start Monday. Welcome to FemFirst." She leaned across the table and shook his hand.

Ms Walker slid the standard employment contract and the annexe contract regarding the wearing of only female products across the table. She passed him a gold pen. He scribbled his signature in the box against his name on the contract and annexe. He put the pen down on the top of the paper.

Aretta's eyes narrowed and a thin smile came to her to her tight lips. Her eyes were as cold as the snow plains of the Arctic.

Chapter 12

A worrying success

The crowded café was full of young people chatting and laughing. The hiss of espresso machines buzzed around the walls. Busy baristas from eastern Europe caed out orders in accented English. Many young customers were typing on white laptops with illuminated logos on the lids.

The bare brick wall behind Stephen was power-scrubbed. He nursed a large mug of Americano with hot milk on the side. No, he hadn't wanted a pastry or a cake. He wasn't hungry. He felt a little sick.

What just happened? he thought to himself. He had passed the interview. He had a job. Great. But it came with one giant snag. Stephen cursed under his breath at what he was getting into. Ms Walker seemed pleasant in an old-school way. But Aretta Ademola? There was something not right with her. He couldn’t put his finger on it. He would be working for her so he would find out soon enough.

Rebecca was at work at the infant school so he couldn’t reach her to tell her the news. He supposed it was good he had a job, wasn't it? He had swapped texts with his wife. She had sent a thumbs-up emoji response to his message.

She was dealing with the class of seven-year-old kids and could only spare a split second. Someone had probably pulled someone else’s hair or someone had thrown something at someone.

It was Friday lunchtime and on Monday

morning, he would be working again. Wearing women's clothes. He shook his head at the prospect. He drained his coffee and stood up. It was time to go home. Rebecca would be back late afternoon so he may as well wait for her at home rather than at a trendy coffee shop where he was the oldest by several years. He made his way home.

Some time later, Stephen heard the sound of the key in the front door. Rebecca was home and he felt nervous. He heard her drop her bag on the floor and let out a weary sigh. He waited with apprehension. How was he going explain the attached strings for his new job?

Rebecca poked her head around the door, wide grin on her face. His hands were under his thighs and his arms straight.

"Well done, I knew you'd get the job." She came in, bent down and kissed him on the cheek. She spotted his glum face. "You don't seem very happy? It's great news, isn't it?" She slumped down next to him, pulling a band out of her hair and shaking her head to let her ponytail out.

He looked into her gentle eyes. He had tried to encourage her to wear make-up and have her hair done but she was comfortable with her casual style. She snuggled her slim boyish figure into him.

"Well, I'm proud of you. You succeeded." She kissed him full on the lips.

He pulled away, a thin smile on his lips, a sombre expression in his eyes. "Yes, I got the job." Stephen's voice trailed off, he couldn't think how he was going to explain this.

He wanted Rebecca to respect him again and be happy with his successes. He hadn't had many lately. His stomach turned at the thought of the agreement he'd made with Aretta Ademola. Aretta's face filled his head. There was something odd about her way. He didn't know what it was but on the journey back from the café, he felt drawn to her power. She hadn't shown him any interest, the opposite. She had been cold. Yet there was something magnetic. And dangerous.

"Hello? Stephen? Are you with me?" said Rebecca.

He pulled himself out of his thoughts. He looked away from Rebecca and at his feet. "There's something I need to tell you about this job," he said to the floor.

"What's the problem? You said you got the job, right?"

"Yes, I did, but please let me finish as there are some." He hesitated. "Conditions." He looked back up at her and stiffened."To get the job, I had to accept their unique proposal and a set of strict conditions."

"Right." Rebecca let the word hang in the air. "What conditions?"

"They are odd."

"So you said. Out with it."

The President of Marketing is odd." He looked embarrassed and put his hands on his knees. The kitchen clocked ticked and a car passed by outside.

"They told me I have to understand the

female market." He looked down again, suddenly feeling hot around his neck.

"OK," she said slowly. "And why is it odd, Stephen? It's a job marketing products to women." An impatient note had crept into her voice; she wanted him to get to the point he was avoiding.

He breathed in, long and slow. Here goes, he thought. "They want me to wear female clothes, make-up and perfume in the office."

His head dropped with his dismay at his admission. He looked beyond her and into the back garden. The late summer sun was low behind the fences and green apples hung from a fruit tree at the back of the lawn. The fading memory of a dying summer.

He felt Rebecca staring at him. "Don't be

silly, Stephen, what are you saying?" she said. "That would be illegal, they can't do that. Make you wear female clothes" She sat bolt upright and snorted. "You're kidding me, right?"

"No I'm not kidding. I know it would be illegal. So do they. They made me sign a contract annexe saying it was my request I dress like a woman."

Rebecca stared at him for a full five seconds. "And you signed it?"

"I had to, to get the job." He looked up to explain. "They'll provide all the clothes and products I have to wear. They said they provide gender-neutral women's clothes with trousers and jackets and plain blouses. I'd have flat shoes so it's not too obvious. But. They demand I wear women's clothes."

Rebecca looked to the ceiling, her mouth dropped wide open. Silence continued in the living room as they contemplated the consequences. Rebecca's hand slid across to take Stephen's.

She broke the silence. "Let's think about this logically."

Stephen loved her practicality and sat up knowing that now it had sunk in, she would propose a sensible approach.

"We need the income the new job will bring."

Stephen shot her a startled look. He had expected her to tell them where to stick their job, not to consider the option he wear women's clothing.

Rebecca had composed herself. "I'm sure no

one will notice if the clothes are plain and unisex. We have little choice for now." She folded her arms, her face set on stubborn. "You're going to have to do it. For now. We can keep job hunting and we'll find something else. Something without odd conditions."

Rebecca had accepted his situation, a little too quickly he thought. "Rebecca, would you be happy with me dressed as a woman all day?"

"Not happy, but it's either that or we lose the house and car. We can't afford the payments. If this means you wearing feminine cuts in your suits at work, then so be it," replied Rebecca, more strongly now.

Stephen was not sure whether his wife's acceptance was a good or a bad thing. He wanted her respect and wondered how much she would respect him when he was a junior assistant wearing women’s clothes. He knew Rebecca was a rational and logical woman. Maybe her acceptance was the rational approach.

“Yes,” he said. “I suppose no one will notice a small difference in the cut of my suit or if the buttons of my shirt are the other way around.”

Rebecca added that his short greying hair and male face would override any lingering femininity on clothing. He looked at her and gave her a short peck on he cheek.

“Thank you for supporting me, I guess you’re right as always, Rebecca. Maybe it will work.”

Rebecca smiled back and they cuddled.

“I'll make us a cup of tea, darling,” Rebecca said to him.

Stephen lay in his bed unable to sleep. He turned to look at the digital clock and hit the button to see the display: *Monday 2.06 am.*

A light wind rustled leaves on the trees that lined the silent streets outside the house. He wasn't going to get any more sleep. Images of him wearing a skirt and stockings flashed in his head. This was stupid, he told himself, that was never going to happen. Even, so, the early morning silence grabbed his imagination and exaggerated his fears

Rebecca's deep breathing from next to him indicated the peaceful sleep she was in, unlike him. The dark stillness of the night amplified the worries in his mind about working at FemFirst.

Aretta Ademola entered his sleepy mind. If Rebecca could see her, she would have told him to be careful. Rebecca would use the expression, Aretta will *eat you for breakfast.*

She would, but what a way to go, he thought. A twitch appeared in his previously dormant penis at the idea. The blood started to cascade into his penis as Aretta's image hung in his mind. Her cool hard eyes, her muscled body and tight black dress. Her domineering stare.

Stephen shook his head to expunge Aretta from his mind. Sleep took him and Aretta's image drifted into his dreams. She was touching him, fondling his stomach. Her hand ran down to his expectant penis. Then she squeezed on his balls so hard he screamed out in his sleep.

They both woke. "What is it?" asked a sleepy Rebecca.

"Just a nightmare, dear, just a nightmare.

Nothing I can remember."

They snuggled back down in their bed. The vision of Aretta's eyes burned into Stephen's mind.

Chapter 13

The first morning

The sound of the receptionist's nails typing on a keyboard grated on his nerves. He waited for Aretta Ademola to collect him from the reception area of FemFirst. It was a grey Monday morning and his first day at his new job.

The young receptionist looked bored and avoided eye contact. A stainless steel clock ticked down the seconds to the re-encounter with his new boss.

Stephen read through a female design magazine. It the only option on the glass coffee table in front of the reception sofa. Tick-tock. Countdown.

The whooshing air of a door opening and

squeal of hinges announced the arrival of the whirlwind that was Aretta Ademola. She strode through, full of purpose and underlying belligerence. His body tensed in edgy anticipation.

Stephen stood and forced a tight nervous smile as she approached. He held out his right hand to shake hers. Aretta stopped short and put her hands on her hips. She rested on one leg. He felt a wave of contempt seemed to fly from her face. He pushed the thought away, she had recruited him. She must want him.

"You cannot come into the office until you have changed."

"OK," he said, noting there was also no greeting.

"You will go to the meeting room. Your

clothing is there ready for you to change."

"Thank you, Ms Ademola." He wondered what they had provided. The not knowing was hard.

The receptionist stopped typing and listened with interest. Aretta nodded to her and asked her how her weekend went.

"It was cool, thank you, Aretta," she said.

"Excellent, Julia," said Aretta turning to Stephen. "There is a dark suit and two plain white blouses for you to change into. One of my staff will provide more clothing later in the day so you have sufficient for the week."

The young receptionist glanced up with a broad grin. Her eyes met Aretta's who raised her eyebrows.

Aretta led Stephen into the meeting room.

On entering, he saw the clothing laid out on the table. His stomach swivelled in nervous anticipation seeing the feminine outfit. His penis tingled, a strange reaction, he thought.

"My staff had trouble finding female shoes in size 9, these black ones are all they had."

The shoes were wide with a thick one-inch heel. Girl's shoes for sure but a neutral as could be expected he supposed.

Aretta picked up two packets from the table. "This is a pack of panties and this one is a pack of knee-length pantyhose."

She ripped open one of the packets and removed a pair of pink panties. She placed them on the table.

"Change. I will then take you into the office and introduce you to the team," said Aretta.

His stomach somersaulted again. This was real. He was going to wear female clothes. His penis twitched again and hardened a little. A surprising reaction.

Stephen picked up the pink panties and rubbed them between his fingers. They were fine cotton with frills and lace around the edges in a deeper pink shade. His finger ran over a tiny pink bow on the front. The other panties were in shades of pink and white and some had thin flowery patterns. This was not unisex. He had to put a stop to this now.

"The panties are too feminine, Aretta. You promised a neutral look," he said.

Aretta sighed and rolled her eyes. "What did you expect panties to look like? Boxers?"

"I'm not sure, Aretta," said Stephen

nervously. He peered at the white girly panties in his hand.

"There is no other option," said Aretta. "Remember? Women's clothes as per your contract? End of discussion." Her sardonic reply cut into Stephen's mild protest. "Put the pretty panties and your new clothes on. Hurry, I am a busy woman and I do not have time for debate over something that has already been agreed." She looked at her gold and silver Gucci watch as if to prove her point. She sighed again and looked to the door.

Stephen felt flustered at her casual use of the word, *pretty*. He hesitated, the panties in his hand.

"I selected you because I thought you would have no problem with this. If I was wrong, you may leave," she said.

Stephen flinched at her curt comment.

She moved to the door. "This will not work if you do not leave your masculinity at the door. That was our deal."

Stephen didn't remember the deal being about masculinity, just using their products. Neutral unisex products, not pink panties with a bow.

Aretta clapped her hands once. "Get changed so we can be marketing girls together."

Stephen froze at what she'd just said. *Had she actually said, girls together?* His face reddened and his jaw tightened.

"I can't be a *girl* Aretta, I'm just using the products as per the agreement, not changing gender," he said through clenched teeth. He told himself to not get angry. That would not be a good approach on his first day.

Aretta stood impassively. Her steel blue eyes glared back at him, a hand on the door handle. “You need to understand three things. The first is you are no longer an executive. You are the administration junior. It means you are the office *girl*.”

His mouth dropped open. Girl?

“Secondly, I am the Global President of Marketing. You will address me as Ms Ademola or Madam. And finally, you signed a contract which stated you will wear female products. You signed the agreement. In our environment, you must be one of the girls.”

Aretta let her final words hang in the fraught atmosphere of the room. “And if you do not like that, leave."

A tight pain hit his chest. *A girl?* He hadn't signed up to be a girl. He'd only signed up to wear unisex products. He couldn't afford to leave or challenge her.

"I don't want to leave, Ms Ademola, I want to work here," he replied sullenly." I thought I was wearing unisex clothes." He swallowed. I didn't expect you would want me to be like a girl."

"This is exactly what I want so get used to it, girl." She folded her arms below her large chest. "Before we go any further, you will tell me you are going to behave and be a good girl. We can then move on and get to work."

His penis tingled at Aretta's words and his mind raced. There were no good outcomes to this. He would have to tell her what she wanted to hear and tonight he'd discuss this with Rebecca.

He bit on his lip and looked to the floor. "Yes, Ms Ademola, I'll be a good girl." He continued to stare at the floor. His face turned hot purple and, at that moment, he wanted to hit out at Aretta. But, there was something else. Something unusual coursing through his body, a feeling of pleasure inside his discomfort. It was comforting to have Aretta taking charge, he had not experienced that before. As a man, he'd always been expected to take responsibility. Here was this powerful woman in control of him. That wasn't comfortable but it was exciting.

"Well done. Good girl," she said. "If you continue to behave this way, this will work well,"

Aretta said.

"Yes, Ms Ademola," he said, contemplating she had just called him a good girl again. This was worse than he had anticipated. He was sure Rebecca will not be happy with Aretta calling him a girl.

So," said Aretta. "Remove the male clothes and put your girl clothes on," she ordered. Her face was an emotionless mask.

"Can you turn round while I undress, please?"

"You are a shy girl. I will turn my back if that makes you feel more comfortable."

Stephen shuddered again at the word, girl.

Aretta turned to face the door. He stripped off his clothes as he watched her back. He stood naked, Aretta tapped a foot.

He glanced at the door and out through the small pane of clear glass into the entrance area. He hadn't expected to be standing naked in a room with his new boss on the first morning of his new job.

He pulled on the pink panties. "I have the panties on."

As he positioned his genitals into a comfortable position inside the panties, Aretta turned around. A smouldering look of satisfaction was written on her face.

"That was not difficult, was it?" She widened her eyes. "They are pretty panties. Cute." Her face creased and she leaned forward as if to see better. "You are hairy. I do not like to see hairy girls." She stood up again. "Never mind, another day."

What did that mean?

Chapter 14

One of the girls

Stephen squeezed his eyes tight. He was struggling to keep his erection from expanding further. The panties felt smooth and light. They clung to his penis and balls like a pink skin.

Aretta's gaze skimmed over his body and fell on the lump in his panties. She sniffed and put her hands on her hips. This was a familiar pose, he noted.

He remembered her comment about his hairy legs. They looked wrong against the feminine panties. He pushed the thought away, he had other worries. He pulled up the trousers as past as possible to cover his embarrassment. They had a side zip and were lower on the hip than he was used to.

He looked down to his feet. The trouser legs were wider. He noticed in horror they had a bootleg look. This was not unisex. He had to get on with it. He put on the blouse and buttoned it up. It hugged his slim body but lay loose around his chest.

He tucked it into his trouser waistband as best he could; it was shorter than his shirts. He knew he would be forever tucking it in. the blouse was short, the trousers low.

He put on the jacket. It fitted snugly and was shorter than his male jackets. He wasn't sure he would get away with this. He was sure someone was going to notice these were female clothe. He had no other option for now. He put on the knee-high tights under the trousers and then slipped on the black low-heeled shoes. Everything was plain as Aretta had promised. Whether it was unisex was debatable.

Aretta was reading something on her phone. “You have taken longer than I expected. I do not want this fuss every day.”

She turned and motioned him for him to follow her. She walked out to the reception area. Aretta placed a security card against a reader and pushed against the door to the main office. He followed her in, suddenly feeling stupid in the female clothes.

The office was largely open plan office. Fluorescent strip lighting sat flush in white-tiled false ceiling tiles. Heads swivelled to look up at him from the desks in lines in the room. Two private offices were situated along the back wall.

They overlooked the footpath behind. A glass-walled meeting room ran along the opposite side of the room and looked out to the front.

A young lady in high stilettos and wearing a pencil skirt strode forward. She was gripping a mug with the FemFirst logo facing outwards. She approached Stephen but stopped a few feet away. Aretta stood back leaving Stephen to stand on his own. He felt exposed and silly.

Ms Walker was resting her arms on a desk speaking to one of the ladies. She looked up from her conversation. She made a quick comment to the woman and approached Stephen. She placed a hand on his shoulder. The thirty or so ladies around the hushed office continue to stare. The lady with the mug watched.

"How lovely to see you, my dear. Let me

introduce you to the team. I've been telling them all about you. Everyone is dying to meet you."

Everyone is dying to see the new man in female clothes, he thought.

"It's a pretty outfit," she added, nodding her head approvingly. "An excellent choice by Aretta." Ms Walker then frowned. "I'm sure Aretta will help you to tidy yourself up a little. You have a few rough edges." She picked up one of his hands and inspected his nails. "Anyway, that's all later, dear." Ms Walker nodded to herself again as if ticking off something on a list.

Ms Walker took his arm, turned to face the office and called out as if she were a school mistress."Gather round, ladies, I want to introduce our latest recruit."

She led him to the centre of the office where

the women gathered. Some held FemFirst mugs and took sips of tea or coffee as they waited. A background hum grew as they started to chat. He could tell they had noticed he was wearing female clothing.

Their murmur increased in level. Janet Walker opened her arms. “Good morning, everyone.” Her sharp accent broke through the voices. “Please welcome Stephen Hayley, our new marketing assistant.”

He scanned their faces. Some of the women smiled at him.

“Stephen is FemFirst’s first male employee. He was an excellent candidate brings a wealth of Marketing knowledge to our company.” She waiting, allowing the employees to settle.

“Stevie had a brilliant idea and this clinched

the deal for us. It was his flexibility of thought that allowed us to recruit a male. He wanted the role so much he offered to integrate with our policy. He understood our policy of femininity and he wants no special favours. He requested he use the same female products as the rest of us. As you can see."

Ms Walker stood to the side a little and waved a hand by his side to display his outfit.

"Of course, we waived the no-trousers rule for him. In light of his decision, we couldn't expect him to wear a skirt, could we?"

A ripple of chuckles greeted Ms Walker's comment. The lady who had earlier approached with the mug said. "Why ever not?"

There was more laughter. Stephen was horrified at first but, as he scanned the group of women, he saw they appeared to be comfortable. He considered that the female product-only rule possibly wasn't a bad idea. They appeared to be appreciative.

He saw Aretta leaning against a wall behind everyone. She was scowling. He didn't see what her problem was, he had conformed to her rule and the team seemed happy.

Ms Walker stepped away and went to stand with Aretta at the back of the room. They huddled for a moment in serious conversation.

The ladies surrounded him. They chattered at once, saying welcome and how great it was to work there. One lady kissed him on the cheek. They were all dressed in expensive clothing with professional makeup.

As the group broke up to return to their

work, Aretta approached him. She tapped him on the shoulder and wagged her index finger at him. “Follow me.”

He felt a moment of irritation at her high-handed manner. He shrugged and followed, it seemed to be her way.

She walked ahead of him. He watched her toned backside moving from side to side. She wore a fitted black dress to her knees. He blinked and tore his gaze away. He was to be working with a team of beautiful women, he couldn’t ogle them all day or his job would end quickly.

Aretta led him to two desks at the edge of the office. They faced each other outside one of the private offices. Alongside the entrance to the private office was another desk. It was empty. A sign on the office door proclaimed:

Aretta Ademola

President of Marketing

She stopped by the two desks. A young dark-haired lady had followed them. She still held her FemFirst mug. It was the lady who had approached him when he first arrived.

"This is your desk," said Aretta. "You will work with Anne. Anne reports to me and she will explain how things work here."

Aretta held out an arm to point to the dark-haired lady. Anne was younger than Aretta and with a shorter and a stocky build. She had a halo of brown hair in a long bob with a fringe. She had a kind tanned face with enormous brown eyes. She didn't have the exotic stunning beauty of Aretta but she had her own pleasant and sexy innocent style.

As with everyone in the office, her rounded sexiness was aided by expensive clothing. She wore a loose flowing dress cut to just above her knees with high-heeled shoes. Stephen wonderedhow he could walk in them. She seemed to have no problem.

"Anne is your line manager," said Aretta.

This was the first time she had mentioned he wouldn't be working for her. He supposed that shouldn't be a surprise, he was the most junior person there.

Aretta went to leave but stopped. "When you've had the chance to settle, I will call you to my office. We need to smooth out some of your rough edges as soon as possible." Aretta turned and marched into her office, slamming the door shut behind her with a trailing hand.

"Nice to meet you, Stevie," said Anne smiling broadly, "That's a cute suit, you look nice. I'll show you the routine and brief you on our projects and our customers."

A friendly smile lit up her face and Stephen felt some of his tension drain away. Anne was far nicer than the arrogant Aretta Ademola. Anne explained they were waiting for another new employee to join, Aretta's new secretary. She would be starting tomorrow.

"It's all change around here," said Anne. "First Aretta, now you and next the new secretary."

Stephen sat down at his new desk. He caught a couple of the other women watching and they looked down rapidly to avoid eye contact. They sniggered to each other.

Anne pulled a seat around and sat next to him. She was nice, he thought.

Anne showed him how to log in to the office network and he felt himself settle. With Aretta shut away in her office and him working with Anne, this looked like it would be fine.

Chapter 15

Feminine steps

Thirty minutes had passed when Anne's phone rang. She took the call and muttered, "Ah ha, of course, Aretta," and replaced the receiver.

"Aretta wants to see us. Now." Anne bobbed her head from side to side and looked at the ceiling in mock anguish. "She who must be obeyed."

They got up and went to Aretta's closed door. Anne knocked and Aretta called out, "Come in." They went in, Stephen following behind Anne. Without looking up from her desk, Aretta told him to go to the kitchen to bring some coffee for their meeting.

Stephen went to the kitchen area and used

the vending machine. He was in good spirits. He had prepared himself mentally for the menial tasks. He had to get on with it. He reflected how he used to have his own administration staff to get his coffee. But this was was easy work for a good salary.

Even so, it was demeaning to be the admin. person after so many years as a senior manager. He hoped he didn't come into contact with his old colleagues. That was unlikely, this was a different market. He hoped. He made the coffee using the vending machine.

He returned to Aretta's office aware of the women in the office watching him. Aretta and Ann sat around a small coffee table. Two chairs were vacant opposite. Aretta indicated he sit in one of them without looking up from a document.

Anne squeezed her eyes up at him in friendliness. He was grateful to be working with someone friendly.

Aretta dived into the meeting topic without any introduction. “Your appearance requires improvement. It is not working. A short hairstyle is unsuitable. We have to use our client’s hair products. A short haircut will tell you nothing.” Her face was set hard. “You will grow your hair longer. You must not cut it until I give permission. Do you understand?”

Aretta jotted at note on the document with a slim silver-plated fountain pen. She looked up. “I am making notes and I will send them to you so we are clear about what you need to do.”

Stephen nodded. Longer hair was no problem. He had never nibothered with any kind of hairstyle before. This would be a nice change. “OK, Ms Ademola.” He crossed his legs and the wider bottoms of his dark suit trousers flapped against the coffee table. He frowned at the buckled shoes he was wearing. They now looked more feminine on pantyhose and with wide-bottomed trousers.

Aretta glanced at his hands. “Your nails are not well cared for. Grow them longer and file the ends. Appearances are important.”

He studied his nails. They were short and not well maintained. The ends were uneven. She had a point. “Yes, Ms Ademola, that will be no problem.”

Anne smiled and Aretta grunted. “We have a beautician who comes in weekly. It is a service the company provides free of charge as part of the remuneration package. Anne will make an appointment for you and the beautician will improve your hair and nails."

Stephen asked, "Is this a female beautician?" He fidgeted in the chair losing some of the earlier confidence.

"Yes," she replied sternly.

He thought that if that made her happy, he guessed there was no problem."I guess that's not so bad, it might be nice to be a little tidier." He smiled at Aretta in a friendly way but she ignored him. Anne raised her eyebrows at him, a smile fixed on her wide lips.

"Something else I noticed," said Aretta. "You slouch when you sit, legs splayed like a man. I want you to sit up straight and either close your legs when sitting down or cross them as you are now. This is about appearances. Women are more stylish than men, more gentle and sophisticated in their movements." She looked to Anne. "I want you to oversee these improvements."

Anne nodded. He had no problem with Anne working more closely with him. She was lovely, he thought. As if reading his mind, she leaned across the table and touched his arm. He blushed.

"Very good," Aretta said, "We will help you to be more like a girl." She grinned broadly followed by Anne.

Stephen's face dropped at hearing the word *girl* again, especially in Anne's presence. He was surprised she didn't appear to think it odd.

Aretta continued, "I have had many years of

experience helping men to improve themselves."

"Yes, Ms Ademola, thank you" he replied wondering exactly what she was talking about. He went to get up.

Aretta slapped her document on the small table. "Did I dismiss you?"

He sat down.

"There is one more item to deal with." Aretta sat back and linked her fingers. A sneer grew on her lips.

He didn't like her look.

"I do not like your name. Stephen is too masculine for our office."

This was an odd thing to say, he thought. This conversation was going in a weird direction. "I'm sorry but it's the only name I have."

Aretta's face looked like thunder. "Do not try

to be funny with me."

"I wasn't, Ms Ademola. I'm sorry." He felt uncomfortable at her tone.

"You need to find something more appropriate for use in the office. Something feminine. You don't have to answer now, think on it overnight. Tomorrow you will let me know what you have decided."

A feminine name? This was going too far. "Stevie can be a girl's name so it works as neutral."

"I don't like it. Find something else." Her face softened for the first time. "I am prepared to give you all the support you need to be successful in the female marketplace. I am only asking for small changes. We have made concessions for you and I ask you extend these concessions to us."

That sounded reasonable on the face of it but he had agreed to wear female clothes. That was a big concession to get this job. "I guess so, Ms Ademola," he replied uncertainly. "You want me to find a female name to use?

"Yes." Aretta stood. The meeting was over.

"I'll talk to my wife about it."

"Good girl."

Stephen's body tensed. He glanced at Anne expecting her to look shocked but she was smiling as if she hadn't heard what Aretta had said.

"You can go." Aretta waved her hand towards the door.

He left her office with anger building at Aretta calling him a *good girl* in front of Anne.

He vowed to avoid Aretta as much as possible and stay close to Anne.

The rest of his first day went in a blur. Anne patiently took him through all he needed to know about working at FemFirst. Spending time with the friendly Anne, helped him to forgot Aretta's jibe.

By the end of the day, he had got used to the clothing he was wearing. Everyone else was dressed in skirts or dresses so he was different.

As he changed out of the female clothing at the end of the day, he thought maybe this was going to work out. Except for Aretta's odd instruction. The feminine name.

Chapter 16

A good girl

"Aretta called me a good girl," complained Stephen. He chewed sullenly at the dining table. Rebecca sat opposite. "She told me to grow my hair and nails and sit like a woman."

Rebecca speared a piece of broccoli. "It's better than calling you a bad girl." She put a finger to her mouth and giggled silently.

"This is no laughing matter, Rebecca," Stephen said.

Rebecca giggled out loud for a second before she stifled it. She pulled herself together.

"I'm not a girl," he added, feeling hurt. His lips tightened.

Rebecca rested her knife and fork on the

edge of the plate. She put her chin on her hands and leaned forward. "Are you saying there is something wrong with being a girl?" Her eyes widened.

Was she teasing him? "That's not what I meant. I'm saying I'm not a girl, I'm a man."

She picked up her knife and fork again. "They are being inclusive. Don't be so touchy. To call you a good girl is a nice thing to say."

This was not the support Stephen had expected. "Are you serious?"

She looked serious. "You're not seeing what I see. You're too close to things. They've taken you into their female-only world and changed their rules for you. You should be grateful. More importantly, you have a job and you're earning a salary again. You should be happy they have tried so hard to find a way around their company rules for you." She returned to eating her dinner thinking the matter closed.

Stephen had lost his appetite. "That's not all. I haven't finished. Aretta told me to find a feminine name for the office. Don't tell me that's normal and inclusive." Stephen was agitated at the direction the conversation had gone. He had expected he could moan about his situation and she would sympathise with him. Instead, she had sided with Aretta.

"That's wonderful," said Rebecca.

"Excuse me? I said they want me to use a girl's name in the office."

She slammed her cutlery down. "I heard you. You should think yourself lucky to have found caring employers in this difficult employment market. You're an older man and it's not easy to find work. We know that." Rebecca sat back, rocking her dining room chair on two legs.

"You believe this *good girl* and *female name stuff* is normal?" asked Stephen.

"No, not if I'm honest, replied Rebecca. "They're trying to make you feel comfortable and closer to your colleagues and customers. I understand why you're not seeing it, you're too fixed in your ways. Being called a girl is not something you're used to but I'm sure they mean it in a kind way. Remember, you're no longer a senior manager, that's gone and you'll never get it back. There is no other option for you. Stephen, why can't you go with the flow and do what Aretta asks?"

Stephen hesitated and thought. His wife was going along with their strange approach. "So, what do you suggest?" He continued in a more circumspect way.

"We should come up with a new feminine name for you," Rebecca said, a serious look on her face. She took another mouthful of her food and chewed slowly.

Stephen looked at her aghast. "It's not my new name; it's a name Aretta wants me to use at work," Stephen said, sulkiness flowing into his voice.

"Whatever," she replied, standing up and looking down on him. "This is an unusual situation but we have little choice. We need the income from this job. I want you to go along with what Aretta asks. It can't be so difficult wearing female cuts in your clothes."

Rebecca was always the practical logical one. He usually liked that, but this was not the time or the situation for trying to be so logical. He wanted her to be outraged at Aretta's behaviour.

"After all that time without a job, you've found a good well-paid position. There are people there who want to invest in developing you. And all you do is complain."

He realised Rebecca was telling him off and thought he was acting badly.

Rebecca said. "Your new girl's name is obvious. Stephanie."

"Stephanie? Are you crazy?" he shouted out, his voice rose in pitch.

"It makes sense, Stephen to Stephanie," Rebecca replied as if this was an every day conversation. "Go along with it but leave it at the office." She thought a moment. "Stephanie? I like it."

"No, you can't be serious?" His bottom lip pushed out like a petulant child.

Rebecca started scraping his plate contents onto hers. She looked down at him as she scraped. "Go along with it, what's the harm apart from your bruised male ego,"

He had no choice. Rebecca was not supporting him.

"Stephanie?" Rebecca repeated, letting the name echo around her head. "It could be shortened to Stephie and that sounds like Stevie if you say it quickly. Anyway, being called a girl and by a girl's name is a small price to pay for our financial well-being, wouldn't you say?"

“I suppose so,” he grumbled back.

Chapter 17

A girl's name

"What female name have you decided on?" said Aretta.

He had just arrived and sat at his desk when Aretta spotted him. She came out of her office to stand over him.

A small pretty young lady watched from the desk outside Aretta's office. Stephen hadn't seen her before.

"It's sweet you want a feminine name, Stevie," said Anne. "Tell us." She leaned across the desks and touched his arm. She slid her chair around the desks to be next to him. Her shoulder touched against his. She moved her face into his, noses almost touching, lips a hair's breadth away.

Her light perfume made his head feel light. And enhanced his rapidly growing desire for her.

Aretta said nothing, allowing Anne to probe.

"Come on, tell us. Don't be shy. What girl's name do you want us to call you?" giggled Anne. She took his hand. He felt her soft palm in his and her thumb stroking the back of his hand.

Aretta stood over him, arms folded. The new secretary watched, her wavy long brown hair was thick and she had large wide brown eyes. She wore a satin effect pink flower in her hair on a clip. It held her hair away from one ear. Her lipstick was bright red and matched her red long fingernails She showed no emotion.

Stephen was flustered. "I discussed it with Rebecca but I think Stevie works. Can't we stick with that? It's a unisex name."

"Yes, you said yesterday but Aretta doesn't like it," said Anne.

Aretta tapped her foot on the floor.

"What did Rebecca say?" said Anne. "I'm sure she thought of a pretty name for you, she sounds like a lovely lady. Come on, out with it, I know you have something in mind." Anne was pushing him to admit it. She knew he was holding back.

"We do not have all the day to wait for you to tell us," said Aretta. The secretary continued to look on with interest.

They were not going to give in, he was going to have to tell them what Rebecca had suggested. He had to remember Rebecca's point it would stay in the office and about the need for his salary.

He looked at the floor. "Rebecca thought Stephanie was the obvious choice. She said it sounds like Stephan so it's not that different. She said you could use Stephie for short, which was like Stevie."

He wished he hadn't blurted out the last part but Anne stroking the back of his hand with her thumb was distracting him.

"I approve," said Aretta. She stopped tapping her foot. "Your wife is a sensible lady. I will ask my new secretary to send an email to everyone to let them know you prefer to be called Stephanie. This is excellent progress. Stephanie."

Anne held his hand tighter and put her other hand over his. She asked him how Rebecca felt about things.

"Rebecca said you were being kind to me,"

he answered.

"That's so cute. Stephie," exclaimed Anne.

She let go of Stephen's hand and hugged him hard. She planted a kiss on his cheek, brushing the edges of his lips. At that moment, he wanted to kiss her, forgetting about his new name. He wanted to immerse his tongue in her mouth. He composed himself, that was not going to happen. The feeling had come over him like a powerful wave. It surprised him by its power. He was falling for her.

Anne let go and ran both her hands down his body to the top of his legs. He twitched as her thumbs stopped an inch or two from his penis. She held her hands at the top of his legs. She let go and sat back, putting her hands on his knees. He wanted those hands on his penis and caressing his balls. Stephen felt a sharp and instant tingle from his penis.

Aretta walked back towards her office. She stopped at the doorway. “Anne, Stephanie, come to my office at 2 pm sharp. We need another meeting.

Stephen nodded but his mind was elsewhere, thinking of Anne. He had to stop this. He therefore decided to say hello to Aretta’s pretty new secretary. The benefit of this job, he mused, was being surrounded by attractive women. Anne wasn’t typically pretty but hell was she sexy. Aretta’s new secretary was small and more delicate than Anne but had something sexual about her. A naive innocence.

He strolled up to her. “Hello, my name is Stephen,” he smiled and held out his hand to shake hers.

The secretary stood and held out a slim limp arm.

"I'm Carla," she replied in a high pitched voice with a strong Spanish accent."I am from Madrid. I worked there for Aretta in her previous job."

Stephen nodded. She was small and young but sexy.

Carla continued. "I recommend you use the name Aretta asked you to use. She is not a woman to accept challenges to her authority. Stephanie."

Stephen mumbled a thank you and returned to his desk. After going through his emails for thirty minutes, an email announcement pinged across the screen. It was from Aretta Ademola,

President of Marketing. He opened it.

To: All at FemFirst

From: Aretta Ademola.

Subject: Our new Marketing Assistant

Dear All

You've all had the chance to meet our new marketing assistant. Our new assistant is keen to integrate, to fit in with our philosophy and to adopt the ethos of our agency.

With this in mind, our new assistant has asked me to inform you we should use the name **Stephanie,** *rather than Stephen.*

Stephanie wishes to be one of our all-female team and also asks we use the pronouns **her** and ***she*** *when speaking about and to her.* ***She*** *told me you may shorten* ***her*** *name to* ***Stephie.***

Finally, ***she*** *wants you to think of* ***her*** *as one of the girls. She asks you refer to her as a* ***girl****.*

I'm sure you'll agree wholeheartedly to ***her*** *request for this and that* ***she*** *demonstrates a wonderful attitude and excellent team spirit. Well done, Stephanie, this is a great initiative.*

Go girl!

Aretta Ademola

Global President of Marketing

FemFirst Inc.

"That's wonderful," said Anne. She glanced up

from her screen. “You are a lovely person to throw yourself into the job like this. I’ll be happy to do as you wish, Stephie, you are a lovely girl.”

She got up and came to Stephen’s side of the desks. She threw her arms around him and gave him another big hug.

His body stiffened. He said, “If you recall, Anne, I didn’t tell Aretta I wanted you all to call me *Stephanie.* It was her idea I have a girl’s name. I certainly didn’t ask to be called *she* or *her* and especially not a *girl.* We never discussed that. And what’s with all those bold and underlined *hers* and *she*? What's that about? You were there, you know this isn’t true.”

“It’s what you wanted and that’s what counts,” replied Anne. “You’re shy and Aretta assumed it’s what you wanted because she knows you're so keen to be part of the team. She has her ways." She kissed him full on his lips holding her closed mouth to his for longer than a peck. She broke off and stood back beaming with an enormous smile.

His eyes remained closed with puckered lips for a split second after she had withdrawn. He waited for more. He opened his eyes and composed himself feeling embarrassed. Her kiss had stopped him complained but things were going from bad to worse.

Despite the madness with female clothing and names, Anne was proving to be something more than a work colleague, even though she seemed a little naive to think he actually wanted this feminisation. He'd been married to Rebecca for over twenty years and although he loved her, things had become stale sexually.

At that moment, he spotted Ms Walker striding towards him. Her eyes were fixed on him. “This is wonderful news, Stephanie. A first-class attitude if I may say so. Well done, good girl. It’s refreshing to find a man who can embrace their feminine side.” She slapped him on the back. “Excellent, Stephanie, this is going better than I expected.”

She marched off leaving Stephen open-mouthed. He looked around him, his face reddening with embarrassment. Carla looked on and said, “This is the beginning.”

What did she mean? The beginning of what?

Chapter 18

Bras and makeup

Anne and Stephen sat in Aretta's office. Aretta was finishing a phone call with a client.

Stephen looked out through the glass door at Carla. There was something odd about her, he thought. She was too girlie with too much pink. He had seen her walk to the photocopier, a dainty girl but with a less than dainty walk. It was more of a male style. Carla's long hair had a large pink ribbon tied at the back. She wore a tiny pink tartan pleated skirt, no more than six inches long with long pink fingernails. He had spotted pink bows at the top of her white stockings. She looked more like a fantasy schoolgirl than the secretary to a Marketing

President.

Aretta put the handset of her phone down. Stephen came out of his trance about the inappropriately dressed Carla and turned to face Aretta.

“Something is still not right, Stephanie. Your clothes are not working as I had hoped. What do you think, Anne? She needs to look more like the girl she wants to be.”

“I don’t want to be a girl.” Stephen started.

Anne spoke over him. “She shouldn’t tuck her blouse in. Girls often wear them outside their trousers.”

Stephen sat up in indignation, “I’m not a girl.”

They ignored him, both in thought.

“You are correct, Anne. Stand up and untuck your blouse, Stephanie."

Stephen pulled the blouse tails out, it seemed a minor point. It kept falling out anyway and it was more relaxing this way.

Aretta peered at him. "The white blouse is too plain. Most of our client's ranges are colourful. I have been thinking about this," said Aretta. She got up and went to her cupboard. "Men wear pink shirts all the time, this change will not make a difference to your neutral look." She handed Stephen a pastel pink blouse. "Put this on and leave it hanging outside your trousers."

Stephen turned the blouse around in his hands. It was bold pink. Aretta was right, men did wear pink shirts. But even so, this looked feminine.

“There is another problem,” added Aretta. “Women wear bras and without this you cannot understand how women feel.”

“Bras?” Stephen exclaimed. He looked back and forth between the two women. He may as well have not been there.

Aretta pulled a white bra from her drawer, raising it in the air with triumph. He noted she said she had thought about and prepared this.

Aretta told Stephen to put the bra on. She laid it on the table along with two items shaped like small breasts. Stephen hadn’t noticed Aretta pick them up.

“They are small A size inserts. They will give you the feeling of breasts for your work. They are not so big that they will show. Much. It’s a neutral change. As we agreed.”

Stephen looked on, his alarm turned to horror. “A bra is not a neutral item, Ms Ademola.”

Anne placed an arm on his shoulder and gave a soft smile. The electricity he felt from her touch dissipated his anger.

“You wanted to wear female clothing, Stephie,” she said. “I know it’s because you wanted to understand how females felt and thought. How could you do that without wearing a bra?” She kissed him on the cheek. “How thoughtful of Aretta to make your new bra as unobtrusive as possible.”

Stephen thought Anne sounded like Rebecca, using logic. He supposed the logic was good but, a bra?

Anne continued. “Stand up and put on your

new clothes. I want to see how they look."

She started to undo his white blouse, standing so close he could feel her fresh-mint breath on his lips and her sweet perfume. Their noses almost touched as he fought the urge to plant his lips onto hers. His penis grew with desire inside his tiny panties.

Anne removed his plain white blouse, her cheek brushed on his lips as she slid it down his arms. She put the bra over his naked chest and clipped it on. He was powerless with desire for her. She picked up the two breast forms and pushed them into the cups.

He looked down at them and felt surprised at the feel of femininity from his white frilly bra.

Anne walked behind him to put the pink blouse on him. She returned to his front and stood close. He wanted to take her in his arms. Her breast touched his false ones. Her lips were a quarter of an inch from his.

He wanted her and felt awful as Rebecca's face came into his mind. Anne finished buttoning the blouse and stroked his face with a soft finger. She kissed his cheek and stood back to admire her work.

He looked down at his body and over two small but obvious mounds on his chest. The blouse wasn't the plain pink effect he had thought. There was a light flower pattern running through it. The flowers were a darker shade of pink with white petals. It had no collars and a lace effect ran down the front. The buttons were a white pearl effect.

"This is better," said Aretta.

Anne clapped once and agreed with a large grin on her face.

“It’s too feminine, it has no collars,” said Stephen. He fidgeted. He saw Carla and one of the other girls from the office watching from outside.

“What’s wrong? I thought you wanted to feel more like the rest of the team. Like a girl,” Anne said.

Aretta joined in the conversation. “If you wear your jacket, no one will see the bra and breast forms. They are small anyway. This is a neutral look. I am not asking you to wear a skirt or a dress so stop comlaining.” Aretta used a brushing away motion with her hand to dismiss the idea.

The mention of dresses and skirts made

Stephen frown. However, she did say they are not asking him to wear them so that was OK, wasn't it? But why say it?

Anne spoke. I have another idea." She left the office and returned with a little nail polish jar. "Don't worry, Stephie, it's clear nail polish. No one will notice you're wearing nail polish but your nails will be tidier. Hold out your hands."

Anne didn't wait and grabbed his hand. She put the polish on each of Stephen's fingernails. Stephen looked at Aretta's glare and didn't resist. Anne finished and gave the bottle to Stephen. "Apply it daily."

He looked at his clear, lacquered nails. They glinted in the light.

Aretta said, "Stephanie, you will wear nail polish every day. It's a neutral clear shade and fits in the policy we agreed. You cannot say clear polish is not neutral."

"The colour is neutral, I guess, but nail polish is not neutral. Nail polish is for girls," he replied

"Yes," replied Aretta. "And you want to be a girl."

Stephen opened his mouth the argue and shut it again. It was no good, Aretta had made up her mind.

"And the final thing," said Aretta. "I do not want you changing in the meeting room any more. It is a meeting room, not a changing room. I am not prepared to block out the availability twice a day."

"Where should I change?" he said.

"You will arrive here as you are now. Female

clothes, bra and nail polish"

Stephen gaped at her but she had already returned to her desk chair to get on with something else.

Stephen sloped from her office. As he passed Carla, he heard her say, "I told you it was only the beginning."

He stopped. "The beginning of what?

Carla raised her eyebrows and looked back at her screen. "You'll see."

Chapter 19

Accepting change

Stephen had his six-monthly review in a few moments. He couldn't believe he had been working at FemFirst for six months.

He had become used to wearing female clothes. Rebecca was less keen. She had become distant over the past six months. It had been her idea and her support had helped him through his time there and the changes he'd had to adapt to. Now she appeared to be unhappy with his appearance and lifestyle at work.

Rebecca accepted his feminised clothing at first, but was now uncomfortable. It started that day he came home in his female office wear. She told him he should have left the office policy at the office. She grudgingly accepted this was no longer possible when he told her of Aretta's demand he turn up in the office in female wear.

At first, she helped him clean off the nail varnish as soon as he got home. It was a chore and they stopped bothering. He now wore it at home too. Rebecca became grumpy and complained she had married a man. Said she didn't know who her husband was; a hybrid man and girl.

She stopped short of making him leave the job. They knew they would be in financial difficulty without the work. Rebecca wanted him to push back at the female product rule. She told him she was concerned by his increasing acceptance of his feminisation. She hadn't minded when he was uncomfortable. Now she thought he was enjoying it. He told her this was nonsense. The problem was, she had a point. He was not about to admit this to anyone, especially not his wife.

Rebecca was pleased with his loss of weight, it was the only positive outcome, she said. Apart from the salary. His small male middle-aged paunch had gone. He had a flat stomach and was several pounds lighter. His waist size had reduced by six inches. Aretta had made him focus on his weight over the past few months.

Stephen assured Rebecca things would go no further. Aretta had only made small changes over the six months, mostly to the colours of his clothing. Of course, his hair had grown and his nails were longer and shaped.

Rebecca warned him to be on his guard.

Women like Aretta were never satisfied.

Chapter 20

Pretty girl

Stephen and Anne were sitting together in Aretta's office around the small coffee table. The six months had gone by fast. Aretta wanted to chair his six-month review.

Stephen crossed his legs. He was suddenly aware of the movement was feminine. Their work on him was getting through, he mused. He was wearing a deep pink blouse with a frill down the front. It was buttoned to the neck.

His suit was light grey with a small flare at the bottom of the trouser leg. Aretta had provided two new suits in addition to the original dark ones: his grey one and the other was pastel blue.

She had given him with a second pair of shoes. They were tan with a slim one-inch heel and a shaped front. Kitten heels, Rebecca had called them. Stephen had protested to Aretta about the shoes. Aretta had acknowledged they were a little more feminine but pointed out he needed to understand how it was to walk in heels. How could he possibly understand how to market heels if he had never experienced them? She had a point. She won the debate. Again.

Aretta had stopped changing his clothes and appearance about four months ago. He assumed it had gone as far as it was going to go. He relaxed into his new more feminine style. This is when the problems had begun with Rebecca. He had stopped complaining about being feminised.

He was using the new hair removal product

the agency was promoting. He had, like all the employees, used it to remove his body hair. Another *minor* change, Aretta had said. Aretta had asked Anne to check his legs every week and occasionally his chest to ensure they were smooth.

His chest mounds were more obvious now. Aretta had changed the breast forms to a B cup. She told him he had to feel what it was like to have breasts. The smaller ones didn't give him the right feelings she said. They were obvious, especially as he had to sometimes go without a jacket now it was warmer.

His hair was now shoulder length. He had kept asking Aretta if he could have it cut as it was longer than Anne's. Aretta would not allow him to have it cut. She provided a hair dye product instead. He had to fit in with the smart corporate identity Aretta informed him. Rebecca had been horrified.

"You can't say dying your hair brown is not a neutral thing to do, everyone does it," Aretta had said.

Rebecca helped him dye it the first few times before she became more unhappy with the changes. He now did it himself. Rebecca also called him Stephie at home but he was unsure if she was being ironic or snot. He was surprised at Rebecca's anger, after all, it was her logic that had persuaded him to take the job with the conditions.

His nail were about a quarter of an inch above the top of the finger. Anne often filed and shaped them for him and painted the nail polish on. She changed the clear nail polish to a pearl shade. Stephen had pointed out it looked like a faint pink but Anne insisted it was pearl.

Aretta liked this small development. She had waved away his protests saying it's not red or pink so therefore it's neutral. Stephen had tried to point out that nail polish wasn't neutral, neither were long nails. Aretta wouldn't listen and, as usual, she won the debate. He had long pearl coloured nails.

Aretta sauntered to the small meeting desk and sat opposite Stephen and Anne. "Before we talk about your performance, Stephanie, I want to talk about your hair," said Aretta. "It needs styling."

Stephen's hand went to his head and stroked his long hair. It had a side parting that sometimes fell across his face. It was annoying so a tidy up seemed a good idea. “Of course,” he said, “I’ll get it cut.”

“Not so fast. Anne will arrange that for you.”

Anne was holding a black-handled hairbrush. She stood up behind Stephen and started to brush through Stephen’s hair. How had Anne known Aretta would need her to do his hair?

“Before I get a stylist to look at your hair, I’ll style it a little for you,” Anne said with a happy voice. She brushed it through.

He closed his eyes as the brush wove through his hair. The points of the bristle massaged his scalp. Anne’s hands stroked his head after the brush had passed through. He closed his eyes and let her brush. This was pure pleasure.

“This side parting has to go, it’s untidy,” said Anne as she carried on brushing. She brushed some of his hair forward from the top of his head and over his face. It came down to his chin.

“Your fringe is too long, hold on a minute.” Anne picked up a pair of black-handled hairdresser scissors.

Stephen looked at her confused, why was she so prepared?

“I’m going to trim your fringe a little. Hold still, Stephie.”

Before he could resist or say anything Anne had begun to cut at his fringe. She trimmed it to below his eyebrows. He felt it tickle his eyelashes.

Anne stood back. “That will do until a hairdresser can style it.”

She brushed the rest of his hair back from the middle of his head and pulled it back tightly.

“What are you doing, Anne?” he asked.

He heard her chuckle. “I’m making it tidy. As Aretta asked.” He felt her twist a band into his hair.

He threw his hands to the back of his head. She had given him a girl’s ponytail high on the back. It hung to the base of his neck.

“I can’t wear a ponytail like this.”

“Nonsense, Stephanie.” Aretta cut across his complaint. The girls outside watched through the glass door. “Lots of men have ponytails, footballers and musicians for example. There is absolutely nothing unusual about a man in a ponytail.”

“Footballers and musicians don’t wear pink

blouses and a bra." He could also feel the fringe just above his eyes. His eyebrows were covered. "Nor do they have a fringe to their eyes."

They ignored his protestations and inspected his new style. Anne touched his hair and nodded.

"Use something to stop it falling out, Anne. I do not want to see Stephanie's hair untidy any more. We run a professional office. Appearances are important," said Aretta.

Stephen felt Anne tying something else into his ponytail.

"Hold still, Stephie, I'm making sure it stays tidy," she said with concentration in her voice.

He turned his head to one side. He felt his long ponytail swinging from side to side and touching against the back of his neck. It was pleasant but he wasn't going to tell them.

"This feels like a girl's style, I can't go out in this."

Anne walked back to face him and gave a big smile. She kissed his cheek, surprising him. "You look pretty. I'm so proud of you."

Stephen felt his penis tingle at her praise.

"This is better, Anne," added Aretta. "The problem is I can see her bare ears. To plain. She needs earrings."

"What?" said Stephen. "What do you mean, earrings?"

Aretta ignored him. "We have a range we market. I am sure there are some samples. Anne, see what you can find."

"No, absolutely not. That's a step too far. Besides, I don't have pierced ears." As he whined, he put a hand to his new ponytail. It was tied with a large ribbon. He explored with his fingers. Anne had tied it in a large bow.

"What's this Anne?" he said.

"It's a ribbon, silly." Anne sounded as if she couldn't believe Stephen was asking. ·"It's to make sure your hair doesn't fall out."She tapped him on the arm.

He peered at his reflection in the glass of the office wall. The two girls behind were giggling. He saw Anne had tied a pink ribbon in an enormous bow at the back of his head.

He felt hot with embarrassment They were going too far. He spotted Aretta signalling to Carla to come in. "Please, Ms Ademola, Anne, this bow is too much. I can't look go anywhere looking like this," pleaded Stephen.

Aretta's face dropped into anger. "Anne has spent the past ten minutes tidying your hair for you and now you are ungrateful? I am not pleased with your attitude, Stephanie"

Carla came into the office carrying a small gun-like device. Stephen looked to her and then to the gun.

Anne stroked his head "Sit still, Stephie." She held the sides of his head.

He was by the three women.

Anne touched his earlobe. "Hold your head still. Carla has done this before. She even did it to herself."

"Did what? What are you talking about?" Stephen was desperate. What was going on?

Anne stood behind him and put both her hands on his temples. Anne leaned in close to one of Stephen’s ears. “You’ll feel a sharp prick in your earlobes but don’t worry it's nothing.”

She stood back and nodded to Carla who put the small gun to Stephen’s earlobe. She pulled the trigger. It clicked and a stinging pain shot through his lobe. As he was reeling in pain, Carla pressed against his other lobe and there was another instant shot of pain. Anne let go of his head.

“That wasn’t so bad was it, silly,” Anne said playfully. “All done.” She stroked his head. “Wait a moment while Carla dabs the blood away from your new earrings.”

“What!” Stephen exclaimed. He shot a hand to his ear. There was a ring with something hanging from it. The other was the same. He pulled his fingers away and looked at a globule of blood between this thumb and forefinger. "You've given me earrings?" Stephen stood up. In shock. "Dangling earrings."

"Yes," said Aretta, disinterested in his complaint.

A smiling Anne held a small mirror to his face. He glared into it. He saw his face framed by a long fringe and dangling silver earrings hanging from each ear.

"I don't want these," he protested, pulling on one. He grimaced at a dull pain from the lobes.

"Anne will bathe your lobe, do not be concerned," Aretta explained. "You will keep them in. I want you to look professional. We have an image to keep up."

Stephen continued to examine the feminine

face staring back at him from the mirror. What will Rebecca say this time?

Aretta returned to her desk.”Excellent, your six-monthly review is completed successfully. This is good progress and I am pleased you look better. Anne and Carla have done an excellent job. You should thank them as without these changes, I would have failed you. And that would have meant I would have sacked you as it was the end of your trial period. I assume you are pleased with the changes and the end of your trial.”

They’d never said anything about a trial period. Stephen looked at his new earrings and hairstyle. He looked up at Anne and Carla. “Thank you?” he said. He felt anything but thanks. Aretta had tricked him again. It was this or fail the trial period he hadn’t been away of.

Anne took his hand. “Come on, Stephie, let’s have a break and take all these pretty changes in. Shall we go out to the new coffee shop in the high street?”

He shook his head. “No.”

“Suit yourself,” said Anne. She took him by the hand and they left Aretta’s office. She guided him towards the kitchen area on the other side of the large room.

“Pretty hairstyle and earrings. Cute pink bow,” called out one of the girls as they walked by.

Stephen looked at the floor, his face burned red. He felt the eyes in the office following his every step. His new earrings jangled against his neck, his ponytail swung as he walked. He understood how a girl felt. It wasn’t so bad.

There was one problem though. He wasn't a girl. On the plus side, he had passed the review and he could settle down to work at the office with no more changes.

Apart from putting him in a skirt, what else could they do to him? And they would never put him in a skirt.

Chapter 21

The summer skirt story

"What do you think of the new summer skirt and sandal range, Stephie? It's our next big marketing project," said Anne.

Stephen was alone in the conference room with Anne. It was great to be out of Aretta's sights. Even a week after the so-called six-month review in Aretta's office, he wanted to be out of sight of everyone else. Aretta made him wear the pink hair-bow, ponytail and dangly earrings every day. She said it was professional for the office. Humiliation was what it was.

He was comfortable with Anne though. Something was blooming with her, at least in his eyes. She wasn't judgmental like Rebecca nor demanding like Aretta. Anne understood he had no choice and accepted him and the embarrassing things he had to wear. She made Aretta's harsh instructions easier to swallow.

He had doubted Anne for a while as she seemed in on the feminisation. Now believed she knew Aretta would get her way so she was making it easier for him.

Rebecca had exploded the evening after the six-month review. He had arrived home with earrings in. Rebecca had hardly spoken to him since that evening. He tried to explain he couldn't remove the earrings when he left the office. The holes would close and he would get in even more trouble with Aretta. Luckily, Rebecca didn't know about the ponytail and pink ribbon, she would have been incandescent. He removed them when he left the office. He was already getting strange looks on the bus home, he couldn't wear a pink ribbon in his hair too.

"Hello, Stephie. Are you here or in another world."

He snapped out of his thoughts. Anne was holding up a short light cotton white skirt, a sunny smile across her face. She wore a knee-length dress and a blouse with no arms. It hugged her stocky frame and large breasts. She looked sexy today, he thought. He looked at her for a moment too long. He imagined her strong legs around his body, her big lips kissing his.

She noticed. "What?"

He shook his head. "Nothing, I was daydreaming.

She waved the skirt in his face. "The skirt?"

It was short, sunshine yellow and lightly pleated with a gathered elastic waistband.

"Pay attention, Stephie, this is the new summer range and it's an important project," she explained. "I need your help to promote it. And your full attention. No more daydreaming"

She held up a few other skirts in different summer colours: white, pink, yellow and pastel blue. A box of white sandals with thick high heels sat on the table.

"The skirt is pretty," said Stephen. He meant it. He imagined Anne wearing it and the two of them wandering by the river, looking for a bar. On a secret date.

Anne had given no indication she was attracted to him too. She must have been 20 years or more younger. But she was always touching his arm, his face, his head. And giving him little kisses on his cheek. He longed for more but it never seemed to transpire. His longing increased now Rebecca was angry with him. It had been weeks since they'd had sex.

Anne slipped the summer skirt over the skirt she was wearing. She undid the skirt and let it drop to the floor leaving the summer skirt. She stood out of it and rummaged around in the box of sandals for her size. She slipped them on. She walked around the meeting room to model it. The skirt was six inches above her knees. The light chiffon flowed against her strong bare legs. He imagined them wrapped around him.

"How does it look, Steph?"

It looked fantastic on her. He had to compose himself. "It has a nice look of summer."

Stephen thought about how sexy she looked in it. He stared at her muscular bare legs. A rush of desire shot through him and piqued interest in his penis.

Anne stopped parading around the room and put her hands on her hips. “I’d like to see how it looks, too.” She looked around the room. “We don’t have any mirrors in here. Why don’t you slip one on for me to see then walk around?”

He froze in shock at her words. She stood looking innocent. Did she not realise what she was asking, he thought? A skirt? She was more naive than he thought.

Anne started searching through the skirts on the table. She held up a bright yellow one. “This one should fit you,” she said, a wide smile on her face, her eyes sparkling.

His face screwed into a frown. "I'm not going to wear a skirt, Anne. I'll go and look for a mirror for you?" He shook his head, his ponytail swung in time with the drop earrings in his ears.

"I'd have to stand still against the mirror. I need to see how it swings and moves as you walk. It's just the two of us. Come on, a couple of minutes. No more. I promise."

He gulped at her pleading tone. He wanted to help her but this was a step too far. Anne had been kind in helping him settle in. All she wanted was to work together with him, he knew that. But asking him to put on a skirt? This was too much.

"I'm not wearing a skirt, Anne." It came out a little harder than he meant.

His emphatic response drew a sharp gasp of

dismay from Anne.

Her smile dropped, her hands fell to the table with the skirt still in them, she leaned forward in despair. Stephen thought she was going to cry, she looked devastated at his reply.

"I thought we'd been working together well, why are you taking this attitude with me? If Aretta had recruited a real girl, she would have had no problem putting a skirt on. Maybe Aretta made a mistake choosing you? I thought you'd bought into this." She sniffed, her head down.

Her comments bit into him. He'd upset her. And she had made a good point.

"Aretta told me she chose you for your sensitivity and openness as much as your marketing abilities. Now you're jeopardising the success of my project by not working with me on this."

Anne was making sense. But it was a skirt.

"You know what Aretta is like," Anne continued. "She'll be on my back if I fail. Stephanie? Please?" She looked at the floor and wiped at one eye with a finger. She twisted at the hem of her skirt with the other hand.

He hated upsetting the only person who had been kind and supportive to him. But she was asking him to put a skirt on. There were limits.

She looked up at him. "I told Aretta I wanted to work only with you on this project. The summer range is a big deal for our client and I thought you'd be perfect. They are one of our most important customers. I don't want to have to tell Aretta you wouldn't work with me. I thought we were friends and work colleagues.

Maybe something more?"

She reached out and touched his arm. She ran her finger down his arm to his hand. She grasped it, wrapping her fingers through his. She looked up at him with watery eyes. "I only want to see how it looks and moves. It's just the two of us and it's for a couple of minutes. No one else will see you in the skirt and I promise not to say anything to anyone."

She walked to the meeting room windows and pulled on the strings to close the blinds. Stephen watched her, the light skirt flicking around her strong legs.

She turned and gave a watery smile. Her large eyes appeared to have dropped in sadness. "I hope no one thinks we're up to something naughty." Her teary eyes glistened. She stood and put her hands together as if praying. "Please put it on. For me? As a friend. As more than a friend?"

Stephen didn't move. Anne held up the skirt again, she pursed her lips as if about to blow a kiss. He went weak at her look.

"Five minutes, please? For me? I have to get this right. If not and the programme fails, we could lose one of our best customers. Aretta will mark me down on my appraisal and I may not get a pay rise."

He watched the tears grow in her eyes. One blossomed onto the top of her cheek.

He couldn't take this any more. "Give me the skirt, Anne," he said with resignation.

Her face brightened.

He looked at her sweet almond eyes. "OK,

OK. It's only for you. You can't tell anybody about this."

Anne swept towards him. "Thank you, you're wonderful. Of course, I promise to tell no one. This will be between us. A shared secret."

She kissed him fully on the lips and lingered. He wobbled in delight and his stomach did a somersault. She moved her mouth sideways and opened her mouth slightly. This was the moment. He opened his mouth to take her full kiss and his tongue moved to his front teeth.

Anne withdrew leaving Stephen with his eyes closed, kissing air. He opened them with a start. Anne stood before him, the little yellow skirt held to his face, a broad grin across her face.

"There's plenty of time to relax later. And maybe more?" She lifted her eyebrows twice rapidly.

He felt weak. That was a promise. Of a kind. He snatched the skirt from her in a fake act of annoyance but with a wry grin. He undid the top button of his trousers.

“I’ll turn around,” she said. “This time. Maybe not next.”

She gave out a girlish giggle as she turned her back on him.

He dropped his trousers to the floor and stepped out of them. He stood in white flower-patterned panties and the blouse. She held out the little skirt with one arm. He looked at the back of her head, her bobbed brown hair and her neck. He hesitated in taking the skirt. This was wrong in so many ways. A skirt.

He had promised Anne he would put it on

just for her but he had a moment of doubt. This was wrong.

Anne giggled. “Hurry up, will you?”

He grabbed the skirt from her. It was like holding a feather. He swooned at the thought.

Chapter 22

A pretty skirt for a pretty girl

He closed his eyes. Here goes, he thought. He stepped into the skirt and pulled it to his waist. The elastic waistband snapped snugly.

He opened his eyes and ran his hands over it. His penis twitched. Anne turned around, a wide beam of pleasure on her face. He went as red as the setting sun. The skirt's hemline was higher than on Anne. He was taller.

He felt liberated to have his bare hairless legs on show and fresh air over his exposed thighs. A sudden excitement hit him at the feel of the light airy skirt. His penis jolted in response inside his panties. He walked away, hoping Anne hadn't noticed he now had an erection. He felt exposed. All that stood behind his hard penis was a light pair of cotton panties and a short feather-light skirt

"Walk around, Stephie, tell me how it feels. Is it nice?"

Stephen walked across the meeting room, the tiny skirt waved around his smooth bare thighs. The feel of the skirt was wonderful, it flowed against his legs. The skirt material moved lightly in the air as he walked. His penis surged harder. He felt light-headed, as if the blood had left his brain for his erection.

His penis strained against the tiny material of the panties. They hadn't been made to house an erect male penis. As he walked, the erection threatened to fall out from the small covering. He needed to stop walking but also keep his back to her.

“Walk some more while I’m trying to think of a slogan,” said Anne.

He had to carry on. He tried to walk more slowly. It was no good, his erection popped out from the panties and stood out, erect under the light skirt. It pushed against the front and the skirt wrapped around it. Anne appeared to be too caught up in her thoughts to notice.

“Yes, the material is lovely, Anne. Can I get changed back now?” He needed to stop this before she saw the tell-tale sign of his erection. The chiffon was rubbing against the exposed head of his penis and making him swoon. It was wonderful. But it had to stop.

Anne looked at him quizzically. “Something’s not right.”

Oh no, he thought.

“You need shoes, I can’t get the feel with you padding around in bare feet.”

This was getting worse. She was prolonging his torture of intense pleasure and panic. He stopped walking and turned to avoid her spotting the protrusion at the front of the little skirt.

Anne looked down and searched through the box of shoes. He tied to wriggle his erection back into the panties as she produced a pair of white sandals in triumph.

He stopped and threw his hands to his side.

“What are you doing?”

“Nothing.”

She didn’t look convinced but held up the shoes. The heels were around four inches. He’d never worn anything like that before. Stephen sighed. He'd have to find a way to put them on without her noticing his loose erection.

He sat on a chair to put them on. He caught his erection between his thighs when she wasn't looking. He held the skirt down with one hand as he lifted his foot into the shoes.

How does the skirt feel? I want you to describe it for me as you walk with the sandals."

He got up and walked away from her.

"Can you twirl a little?" she said.

Maybe a twirl would make the skirt go out and away from the erection, he thought?

Stephen moved around the meeting room, weaving through the chairs and back towards Anne. He made little twirls of his hips and bum to keep the skirt away from his penis head. He turned his back to her and twirled from side to side to make the skirt swing around his thighs. His erection swayed under the skirt.

Anne laughed and clapped at his catwalk-type walk. Stephen thought about this ridiculous situation – him performing in a skirt for Anne. What would Rebecca say? She will never know. But this was fine, it was for Anne. He had to keep her from seeing he was hard and excited.

Stephen started to describe the feeling for the marketing campaign and slogans. "It's like the breath of summer, warm sunlit breezes." He swung his hips making the skirt rub against his legs like the soft caresses of a light breeze.

He lost himself in the freedom of the little skirt and the air around his penis. The gossamer-like skirt was brushing his thighs and his erection. His legs felt incredible without trousers enclosing them, imprisoning them. And he was with Anne, supportive lovely sweet sexy Anne.

He held the hem of his skirt between two fingers of each hand. He swayed it back and forth as he paraded around the meeting room. Anne was no longer watching but was typing something rapidly on the screen with two thumbs. He stopped walking.

She looked up. “Don’t stop, I had an urgent message. Won’t be a minute.”

Stephen chuckled to himself. Always multitasking, he thought. He continued to sway his body and his erection swung under the skirt. His mood lifted like the hem of the skirt he was holding up. Anne had become a wonderful friend and maybe more soon. He wanted to please her and repay her kindness. He looked at her smiling face. She pushed her hair back as she put her phone back down on the conference table. She gave him her full attention.

“Stephanie?”

He stopped dead, frozen with his skirt hem held out. She had used his full female name. That was odd.

Anne started to giggle. She put her hand over her mouth. “I can see your penis. It’s hard and showing under the hem.”

He looked down. He’d got carried away and pulled the hem too high. The end of his erection showed. He pulled his skirt over it, his face suddenly burned with humiliation.

“Don't worry, Stephie. It’s cute you’re excited by the skirt. I don’t mind.”

He wanted the ground to swallow him up.

She went to him and wrapped her arms around him. She laid her head on his chest. "I'm so pleased to be your friend. You're wonderful, Stephie."

His erection poked into her stomach.

"Sit down," she said. "I have one more little task to make you look the part. "Don't worry about your excited winky. I've seen it now and besides, we're friends."

She went to her handbag. She pulled out a little clear plastic box while he fought with the skirt to keep his erection covered.

"You need make-up. You can wipe it off later but for now, I want you to look pretty. You've gone this far we may as well go the whole way."

He protested but she told him not to be so silly. As he sat, his lightweight skirt blew up exposing his erection. He went to cover it. She held his hand.

"Leave it, Stephie, it's too much fuss, I don't want you to keep fiddling. I've seen it now and I don't mind. It'll only pop out again. As I said, it's cute.

He didn't think his penis could get any harder hearing her words.

He sat, his yellow skirt resting away from his rock-hard erection. She looked, smiled and screwed her eyes as she mouthed, *cute.* Cute wasn't what he wanted her to say but that was good. Wasn't it?

She made up his face, lining his eyes and painting his eyelids. She dabbed at his cheeks and painted his lips. He adored her attention. She stood back and admired him. He melted with love at her attention.

She glanced down at his erection again. “Do you like being a girl? It looks as if you do. I don’t mind if you do, I like men who are in touch with their feminine side best.”

He coughed, unable to say anything. She liked him feminised. That was good. With the blinds pulled, maybe something more was about to happen. He hoped she’d caress his erection before her mouth engulfed it.

Anne looked into his eyes. “You look pretty,” she whispered.

His body went warm with excitement at her words. His erection throbbed in the chilled air-conditioned atmosphere.

“Very pretty indeed, but you two need to stop what you’re doing. Something urgent has come up."

The voice was cold, searing and hard. The enunciation was precise. It was not Anne's voice.

Chapter 23

Trapped in chiffon

Stephen froze for a short moment. He swung around slowly, pulling the skirt over his erection. He had been lost in his emotions and the sensations of a sexy skirt. He hadn't heard someone enter the meeting room.

His eyes widened in horror. Aretta stood in the doorway. Her face was stormy, her hands were on her wide hips. She dropped her hands and strode to the table, her high heeled shoes clicked on the floor like an invading army. She sat at the head of the table. She flushed out her dress to let it fall around her seat. She sat straight-backed. Her dress front was low and her dark breasts pushed out like huge melons.

Stephen glanced to the door: she had left it wide open.

"Anne, take a seat," said Aretta. "Stephanie, stay where you are. We have an urgent task to see to."

Stephen stared at the open door. He could see some of the other girls at their desks. They hadn't yet looked up but when they did, they'd see him in the little skirt.

He moved towards the door to close it, keeping to one side to avoid being seen. "I'll close this door and then get changed." He dropped his hands to the front of his skirt. This was a disaster. Aretta was there with him in a little skirt. And he had an erection.

"Stop!" said Aretta. "Go to the whiteboard and take notes while Anne and I decide on the approach to this little emergency."

He felt weak. "I was only wearing this skirt for Anne. She wanted to look at it. I'll change."

Aretta cut him off. "I am not interested. We have work to do. Take the marker pen and take notes on the whiteboard," she growled.

His eyes flitted to the open door. He backed away further from anyone's potential eye-line.

"Can I close the door, Ms Ademola? Please?" His voice rose high with panic.

"No," Aretta said, her voice level. "The door remains open. You may change back when we have finished this urgent work. The customer has brought forward their launch date for the summer wear. We need a draft promotion strategy by the end of the day."

Having decided the discussion was over, she

moved on to business. “How do you think we should approach the strategy for this range, Anne?”

“I should change first, Ms Ademola,” cut in Stephen. “And clean off my make-up. I can’t stand here in a little skirt,” said Stephen.

He looked at Anne. She was impassive.

Aretta banged a fist on the table. “Stop this now, Stephanie.”

Aretta stood up. Aretta never lost her temper but he he had pushed too far. She leaned forward across the table, her breasts deep and luscious. “We need to work through this strategy. So, for the last time, stand there like a good little girl and take notes on the board. I said you can change back and clean your face when we’ve finished.”

Her eyes floated over him taking in his new look, an eyebrow lifted. Stephen wanted to curl up in the corner with embarrassment. His bare legs were too exposed, his skirt an embarrassment and his erection a humiliation. It pushed out the front of the skirt. Even with Aretta there. Or maybe because she was there.

Aretta's eyes narrowed. She pointed a long slim dark finger at the front of his short skirt. "I hope that goes down. Disgusting."

He tried to fumble it back into his panties through the skirt

Aretta sat and banged the table again. "Stop playing with yourself, stupid girl. Concentrate on the job." Aretta was glaring.

He was going to have to stand and bear it. The end of his erection floated against the fine skirt material. It was exquisite torture. He felt he was hyperventilating. This was a terrible moment, the worst in his time working here and there had been a few. So if it was so awful, why was he so hard? He tried to calm down by telling himself he could get through this. Aretta was one more who had seen him in a skirt. He would change when they finished the work and the rest of the office would be none the wiser. His breathing calmed a little as he told himself it would be fine.

The only problem with this approach was the meeting room door. It was wide open and Aretta showed no interest in closing it. The girls outside had still not looked up. He had to hope they wouldn't look in. The fewer people who saw him this way the easier it would be to revert to normal wear. Whatever normal was in this office.

The impromptu meeting continued for the next hour. Stephen wrote notes on the whiteboard while his yellow skirt flowed around his thighs. His erection stubbornly refused to go down. His foreskin was fully retracted and every movement made the thin material glide over the exposed end of his penis.

Every time Anne looked up to ask him to write something, her eyes drifted to the protrusion at the front of his skirt. She said nothing but he spotted she had lost her friendliness. Perhaps it was because Aretta was there and she had to be professional. Or perhaps it was her who had told Aretta. Why had she been texting earlier?

He considered this. No, not Anne. It was

probably just a boyfriend. A boyfriend? He hoped not, they were finding something special together. The thought of Anne telling Aretta circulated in his mind and he tried to push it away.

He was struggling to concentrate. Despite the circumstances and Anne's possible betrayal, the skirt felt wonderful against his thighs and erection. He wanted to hold the skirt tighter against his penis and masturbate.

Of course, that was out of the question but he could dream. His sensitive penis head rubbed again and again against the fine material of the skirt. It produced a sensation like a soft feather and made him light-headed. He became worried he would cum if this continued.

Salvation came in an unexpected way after

thirty minutes. "We will take a short break," said Aretta, her mood was lighter than when she'd come in. She sat back in the chair and stretched. His eyes fell against her huge strong breasts. He tore his gaze away.

Stephen put down the marker pen walked to Anne. "Could you pass me my trousers, Anne? I can use the break to get changed."

"What are you doing?" asked Aretta.

"Changing back into my trousers, Ms Ademola, as you said I could."

"I said nothing of the sort. I said you could change once we had finished and we have not finished. We are taking a short break. I want coffee and you will get it for us."

Horror filled him. "I can't go out there, Ms Ademola. I'm wearing a little yellow skirt, high heels and face make-up."

"Who else is going to do it? You're the assistant, not me?" said Aretta. "Run along like a good girl and get our coffee. Anne will look after your trousers. They will not go anywhere."

"But you said I could put my trousers on."

Aretta was no longer listening to him.

Anne stood and touched his arm. Her thigh brushed against his erection. "You look gorgeous. There's nothing to be ashamed about. You have beautiful long legs and you should show them off. You're pretty." Anne beamed a bright smile with wide lips and innocent eyes. Or was it so innocent? Stephen didn't want to look pretty, he wanted to put on trousers and to wash off the make-up. Aretta pointed to the door.

Stephen dropped his head and walked

towards the door. His ponytail flicked against his neck, his earrings clinked. He had no choice, he had to leave the room and get their drinks. In a skirt and high-heeled sandals.

He glanced through the doorway and caught the eye of the lady outside. She smiled and looked down again. Then she looked up, her mouth fell open as she saw his little skirt. He straightened himself and put his shoulders back. Brazen this out, he told himself.

He staggered on in his high heels towards the kitchen area. The short fine yellow skirt waved against his legs, outlining around his erection. He vowed to try to tuck it in once he got to the kitchen.

Everyone stopped talking and all eyes followed him. The sound of someone's stifled giggle rang out.

Back in the meeting room, Aretta sat back and put her hands behind her head. “You've done well, Anne,” she said. “I knew you’d get him into the skirt and heels, he’s besotted with you. It was only because of old Ms Walker’s reticence, I waited this long. I did not want to cause any office strife with her. Just yet.”

The two ladies smiled at each other.

Ms Walker rushed past Stephen as he was using the vending machine. She stopped then turned. She hesitated a moment before walking to the kitchen area.

“This is an interesting development, Stephanie.” She nodded to herself, taking in what she saw.

Stephen froze to the spot not knowing whether to run or scream.

"I love the skirt and sandals. And what beautiful long legs. The make-up is a great touch." She gazed a while longer. She put her hand to her chin and pondered. "We should return to the no trousers policy for the office. I didn't realise for one moment how much you would embrace your work here. Well done, Stephanie, and I'm pleased with your commitment. I'll speak to Aretta and see if she agrees with me about returning to the full no-trousers policy immediately."

She glided off.

Aretta? Agree? It was her who made me do this, he thought to himself.

Stephen's head swam, everything had

happened so fast. He was wearing a skirt and everyone had seen him. At the same time, it was an exhilarating feeling, one he had never expected. The soft material and the feeling of air around his legs and genitals was exhilarating.

He finished filling the coffee cups from the vending machine without thinking and returned to the meeting room. All eyes in the office followed him back as he entered the room.

He placed the cups of coffee on the conference table. Aretta looked at him.

“Can I change back into the trousers please, Ms Ademola?” Stephen said, his voice forlorn and low.

Aretta stared at him, her eyes wide in shock. “What is wrong with you? You are wearing a skirt and this is not a problem for me. You have an erection so you have no problem either. Ms Walker popped her head in while you were making the coffee and we have agreed to reset the no-trouser policy in the office."

Stephen sputtered. "What do you mean?"

"I mean, you have shown you can wear skirts and dresses like the rest of us. I therefore expect you to arrive at the office each morning in a skirt or a dress. The no-trousers policy in the office has been restored." She shook her head. "It is what I wanted to begin with but Ms Walker insisted on a more lenient policy for you. I was correct all along which is no surprise."

Stephen looked to the ceiling. She had checkmated him.

Chapter 24

One step beyond

A yellow-red moon hung low, partially obscured by low dark clouds. Stephen smelled rain in the air as he hurried along the street. He put his head down and strode as well as he could in the white sandals. The street lights gave his short flowing yellow skirt a subtle tone of amber. He kept one hands on the hem to stop it flying up in the damp wind.

He was sure he had been spotted as a man in a dress but no one had said anything. He hoped the neighbours would see only another woman making her way home. He didn't know his neighbours well. He said hello to them from time to time but that was all. He didn’t want to say hello tonight.

As he approached his house, his eyes flitted either side of the road. A young lady was walking a small dog. It was more intent on sniffing the grass verge fro signs of potential partners. No one else was around. A few cars sped past. The drivers didn't notice the tall thin awkward figure in a tiny skirt and sandals with their head down.

Stephen reached his front door as the first spots of rain dampened his thin skirt. He had no erection now, this was too awful. He looked around one more time and the young lady and her dog were walking away in the other direction. A white van went past, the driver peering ahead in concentration. He sighed deeply and let himself in. He had been lucky. He hoped he would be lucky with Rebecca understanding his latest predicament. She had mellowed in recent days. She seemed to becoming used to his feminisation. He hoped she'd accept this latest escalation.

He shut the front door feeling stupid. He was dressed in a little skirt and high-heeled sandals. In public. His fair hair hung around his face and across his shoulders. Rebecca strolled out of the living area and into the hall to greet him. She stopped dead, a smile frozen on her face. Her smile dropped away like melting snow from a spade. Her body jolted tight. She blinked twice.

"What on Earth. Are you wearing?" Rebecca put her hands to her face. He mouth dropped open. She shut it hard, clinking her teeth together. "Don't tell me you came home dressed like that?”

Stephen looked down and nodded. “Aretta made me do it. I think Anne helped.”

“*Aretta made me do it,*” she parroted.

“Rebecca, don’t mock me. They made me wear a skirt and high heeled sandals. I thought Anne was my friend but I think she tricked me,” he rambled.

“*I thought Anne was my friend.*” Rebecca’s voice mimicked his whine again, soaked with sarcasm.

Tears welled in Stephen’s eyes. “Aretta said I have to wear dresses and skirts at work and they won’t let me change there any more. I had to come home in a skirt. I’m not allowed to wear trousers any more. I have and go there tomorrow in a skirt.”

"Stop." Rebecca stood tall, her hands on her hips. She stuck out an arm to the next room. "Go to the living room. We need to talk. Now."

"Let me change first," he whimpered.

"Change? You come home wearing a pretty little yellow skirt and now you want to change? Get in the living room now." A single forefinger pointed to the door.

Rebecca turned and marched out of the hall. He saw his appearance in the hall mirror. A strange pang of pleasure hit him with the surprise at what he saw. He was attractive. He touched his long dangling earrings through his long hair. He swallowed hard and followed his wife into the living room.

Rebecca sat at one end of their wide sofa. It looked out of date with its large attached cushions and floral pattern. He'd never noticed before. It had once seemed familiar and comforting but now seemed as if he was observing as a visitor.

Rebecca focussed on him, her eyes flitted over his skirt and legs with contempt. She blinked and he was surprised to see her wipe away a tear. Yet her face was set hard and expressionless.

"Sit Stephen or is it Stephanie? You look more like a Stephanie to me."

"Stephen," he mumbled.

She grunted. "This has gone too far," she said with a touch of steel in her voice. It was as if she had come to a decision.

"I married a man, not a woman. You look like a woman. A slightly slutty woman with your long thick blond hair and short skirt. It was fun at first and necessary to get the job but I'm not comfortable with where this has gone. Tonight, you've taken it too far. Pierced ears and a mini skirt? That's not normal."

He sat and leaned forward. "But, Rebecca, I can resign."

"You could have done something about this a long time ago. You didn't went along with it and let them to turn you into a girl. I want you to leave so I can get on with my life and find a man. My current man left me to become a girl."

Stephen shook his head. "I had no choice, it was Aretta, she tricked me."

"I suggest you ask Aretta to help you to find somewhere else to live as you're no longer welcome here."

Stephen slumped back in the chair.

"Speak to her first thing tomorrow. You have until the end of the week to get out."

Chapter 25

A sissy life

"Would Mistress Ademola like anything?" The housemaid's voice struggled to compete with the loud classical piano coming from the room speakers. It filled every crevice of the apartment.

Aretta looked up from her smartphone. She had been absorbed in her work. She shook her head, her long straightened black hair shook side to side around a chiselled face. There was not a single line on her dark porcelain-smooth skin.

She wore a tight low-cut leather top. Her breasts fought to escape the restricted clothing. Her thick sultry red lips parted slightly to show a glint of brilliant white teeth. There was no aggression in her manner and no warmth. Her steel blue eyes were sharp and deep like a dangerous ocean.

Aretta watched her new maid with an imperious glare. The maid's long thick light hair was full and flowed over broad shoulders. The maid was slim and willowy. Aretta had put her new maid on a restricted diet since she had come to live and work at her home.

Aretta liked her maids slim as this made them graceful and appear more feminine. She added heavy make-up, black false eyelashes and huge earrings. They never quite lost their male look but that was part of the fun.

The evening sun dipped and glistened on the great river twenty floors below the apartment. It split the city like a rip in fabric. Passing boats left their wake on the river lined by apartments for the wealthy.

Aretta watched her maid’s eyes lower to the floor to avoid her piercing aggressive eye contact. As she always taught them. Aretta’s face twitched at the sense of fulfilment, seeing her new maid dressed in a short pink satin dress for the first time this evening.

She mused at her maid’s enormous D-cup breasts, stretching and testing the dress front. The maid's uncovered smooth light-skinned arms flowed into long wide hands with pink lacquered fingernails. The nails were a quarter of an inch from the tops of the fingers.

Aretta considered herself a benevolent mistress as she always took her maid with her to get their nails done together. Not many employers would do that, would they? This new maid looked as if she would fit in well. She loved to cal them she even though their genitals said otherwise. That was part of the fun, of course.

A brilliant white small pinafore hung around the maid's waist with frills around the edge. The dress flared out from the maid's waist and was so short it didn't cover the maid's penis beneath. Nor the white suspender belt holding up white stockings. Aretta he was happy seeing the smooth light stockings on long slender hairless legs and patent white leather shoes with high thin heels.

This is how all men should be. Submissive and feminised.

Aretta stood and rubbed a finger along Stephanie's jawline. It was like a polished and varnished tabletop. There was not a whisker of hair. She had learned her feminised maids could be careless or lazy. She had taken no chances with Stephanie. She had had all his hair from the neck down removed by electrolysis before starting work. Except for a small triangular pubic hair area.

She hadn't yet told Stephanie she had booked him into a clinic. Aretta sometimes liked her maids to work naked and to play together. Their flat chests irritated her. The clinic would rectify that problem and Stephanie would soon have real D-cups. Not that he knew yet that it was a condition of him living here. Aretta had put him up in a hotel for a few days after his wife had kicked him out. Once she had him prepared, she allowed him to move in as her full-time maid.

Stephanie waited from Aretta to dismiss him.

Aretta mused how she missed having two maids as she'd had in Spain. That would happen although Stephanie didn't know he'd be sharing duties with another feminised maid in the near future. Or a bed. Aretta liked her maids to be 'girlfriends' and to perform for her amusement.

Stephanie had so much to give and such great energy. Stephanie's feminisation was going well and it was time now for the next stage.

Anne stood up from the seat opposite Aretta. Aretta had identified Anne as a future Mistress. It was time for Anne's training to move forward to the next stage after her success in working with Stephanie's feminisation at work. Anne strapped a black leather belt around her hips. Aretta was impressed at how real the seven-inch flesh-coloured dildo looked. It poked out erect from the front of Anne's belt.

Stephanie watched with worry etched in his eyes. He knew they would do what they wanted. Aretta sat back in her chair and waved a hand to proceed to Anne. Anne told Stephanie to turn around and bend over. He did as she had told him and Anne moved towards him from behind. Anne rubbed gel around the tip of the lifelike dildo. Without warning, she thrust it into his exposed bottom hole.

Stephanie squealed and turned his head back. His lips trembled as if he were about to let out a sob. It never came as Anne withdrew and thrust her dildo inside him again in one thrust. He cried out again. Anne withdrew and then thrust it again and the belt slapped against his bottom cheeks

Anne was a good student, she will do well. Stephanie had to endure whatever they decided, there was no other option. Rebecca was a past memory in this new life of his.

Anne finished pegging Stephanie but told him to stay bent over. Aretta watched with approval as Anne removed her strap-on dildo. Stephanie remained bent over, his pink dress laid on his back, his shaved balls hanging between smooth thin legs. His erect penis throbbed.

Anne held a pink butt plug and thrust it all the way in. “That stays there,” said Anne. “Stand up, turn around and lift your dress front.”

Stephanie shuffled around to face Anne. Aretta looked on with satisfaction, the mistress of ceremonies. Aretta held a plastic device in her hand and passed it to Anne. Anne stood before Stephanie.

"Hold your dress higher, girly," said Anne.

Stephanie pulled it up with both hands, exposing his clean smooth genitals. A triangular patch of pubic hair was the only contrasting feature across an otherwise smooth pink mass of skin.

Anne clamped the pink plastic cage onto his cock and around his balls, squeezing it in without any consideration for his stiff bone-like erection. He lost his erection. She pushed his flaccid penis into it and locked it up. The cage was far too small for his penis. She squeezed four inches into a cafe only one inch long.

"Ouch, it's too small?" he said.

Anne slapped his cheek. His head rocked to

one side with the force.

“Don’t ever complain or tell me what to do.” Anne was no longer pretending to be the sweet girl at FemFirst's offices.

“If you must know, I’m shrinking your clitty. Four inches isn’t feminine. I want it down to one inch. Hence the size of the cage, girly. It’ll atrophy when kept squashed away.”

She told him to thank her for the slap, for the anal pegging and for locking his clitty away and for wanting it smaller.

Stephanie looked down and said, “Thank you, Mistress.”

“Good girl,” said Anne. “I will let it out when you have a pretty girlfriend to play with.”

“A girlfriend?” said Stephanie.

Anne squeezed her eyebrows for a moment.

"Yes, but not a real girl. A sissy like you."

Stephanie's mouth dropped open.

Aretta stood from her chair. "Kneel and kiss our shoes, housemaid. Then get up and curtsy."

He knelt and kissed their shoes. He got up and curtsied.

Tomorrow Aretta would take Stephanie to the FemFirst office for the first time since he had come to live with her as her maid. Stephanie's driver's uniform was hanging in Stephanie's bedroom at the other end of the apartment. It was a white jacket with a tiny matching pencil skirt, an inch longer than the jacket.

Stephanie thought he had the double bed to himself. He did for now. That wouldn't last, she needed two maids. They would sleep together and play together. Whether they wanted to or not.

Aretta thought about changing his name. Stephanie was a normal girl's name. It had served its purpose. He now needed a sissy name. Like Candy, Sissy or Polly.

The girls at FemFirst will be pleased to see Stephanie again, thought Aretta. She had found another suitable male to replace Stephanie as Anne's Marketing Assistant. He was a pliable sensitive man too and he looked good in female trousers and blouses. She told Anne they wouldn't wait so long next time to get him into skirts and heels. A month, no more. Two weeks would be better.

Stephanie went to the kitchen to make dinner for the two mistresses. He thought about the turn his life had taken — the transformation from a senior executive to a domesticated and subservient housemaid to a benevolent mistress. His mistress was benevolent as long as he did exactly what she demanded.

He belonged to Aretta.

THE END

Dear Reader,

I hope you enjoyed 'A Very Dominant Lady'. I would love to be Aretta, it would be wonderful to live her fantasy lifestyle.

I'd love you to share your thoughts on the story and post a quick review.

You can also enrol for my newsletter and receive free stories and special offers direct to your mailbox.

Go to my true-life blog at ladyalexauk.com, and sign up. You can also read about my real-life FLR with my husband, Alice

Thank you so much for reading my story,

Alexa Martínez (aka Lady Alexa)

London, England.

Printed in Great Britain
by Amazon

25296232R10172